THE RENOS

The Civil War was over and vast sums of money were being transported to the destitute South. Nobody had robbed the railroads before — until the Renos came along. The five brothers were to become the scourge of Indiana and Missouri. Then a railroad guard got gunned down, and the Renos — who had always been proud of never having killed — were branded as murdering outlaws. Before justice could be done, events would explode into horrifying violence.

WOLF LUNDGREN

◆

THE RENOS

Complete and Unabridged

LINFORD
Leicester

First published in Great Britain in 1999 by
Robert Hale Limited
London

First Linford Edition
published 2000
by arrangement with
Robert Hale Limited
London

British Library CIP Data

Lundgren, Wolf
    The Renos.—Large print ed.—
    Linford western library
    1. Western stories
    2. Large type books
    I. Title
    823.9′14 [F]

ISBN 0–7089–5692–0

Published by
F. A. Thorpe (Publishing)
Anstey, Leicestershire

Set by Words & Graphics Ltd.
Anstey, Leicestershire
Printed and bound in Great Britain by
T. J. International Ltd., Padstow, Cornwall

This book is printed on acid-free paper

Author's Note

This fiction is based on historical fact ... In their brief reign the Reno Brothers robbed more cash from banks and railroads than the James gang even dreamed of.

W.L.

1

They rode their horses through woods turned into a patchwork blaze of scarlet and gold, chilled by the frosts of October, the presage of winter. But they paid no heed to the stark beauty of the wild, deeply chasmed landscape. Their thoughts were on what they were about to attempt that night, the possibility of success or failure, riches or death. They planned to do what no man had done before, the hold-up and robbery of a railroad locomotive, the Ohio and Mississippi Flyer. They were going to make history.

The Reno brothers — John, Frank, Simeon, William, and Clinton — were a close knit quintet who had learned how to ride, shoot and kill in the Civil War, but without any special glory. Their speciality had been bounty jumping, collecting cash by enlisting in

1

the Union army, then deserting and volunteering elsewhere. By guile and bravado they had managed to stay one step ahead of the authorities. At war's end they dabbled in forgery and theft and made a modest living. But now, on 6 October 1866, they were looking for bigger profits.

'That railroad clerk better have been telling me the truth,' John Reno shouted, as he plunged his Morgan stallion down through a gully of embedded leaves and raised an arm to fend off the hickory whips that whapped back at his brothers. 'Or I'll be back to deal with him.'

Big John was the oldest and tallest, and, as such, the natural leader of his brothers. He wore a long canvas riding coat lined with Missouri blanket, held tight by a thick leather belt into which were stuffed twin Remington revolvers, the New Model Army issue of '63, which he had failed to surrender. Like the others he had a widebrimmed campaign hat canted down low over his forehead, covering his black hair.

'You cutting him in?' Frank Reno called.

'Sure, he'll get what's coming to him.'

Unlike his rough-hewn, bearded, older brother, Frank was a bit of a dandy. He sported a gambling man's frock-coat and cross-over vest beneath his riding cape, clean linen, pearl cufflinks, and a diamond pin stuck in his cravat. His pearl-grey trousers were tucked into blood-red boots, and his dark, glinting eyes and jutting black goatee gave him a wild, cavalier look. His preferred arms were a Smith and Wesson .44 in a button-over holster on his belt, and a little two-shot derringer tucked out of sight in his pocket.

'You figure it can be true, that they're carrying ten thousand dollars in the strong box?' he asked as he rode abreast of John.

'That's what he said — ten thousand in the Adams express car and more valuables in the safe.'

'Whoo!' Frank gave a low whistle. 'It's a damn fortune.'

The brothers thrashed their mounts down through a rocky coulée with a noisy clatter of iron-shod hooves and a jingle of harnesses. 'There she is,' John called, as he spied through the trees the curving single track which climbed a gradient not far outside the town of Seymour. 'And there they are.'

He was referring to a huddle of shabby, hang-dog men who were waiting with their scrubby mounts close to the track. 'Don't say nothing to them about how much we're hoping to get.'

The waiting men were mainly youths, ragged and ill-nourished, inbred hillbillies from the woods, one wall-eyed, another hare-lipped, whom they had recruited for extra fire power. They were crack shots with their squirrel rifles and Kentucky longarms, and would as soon cut a man's throat as skin a 'coon.

'Howdy, boys,' John said. 'Glad to see y'all made it. We got work to do.

Which of you's handiest with an axe? I want that big hickory brought down across the track. The rest of you set to tumbling boulders to build up all around it. That Flyer ain't gonna git past us.'

This was a new adventure for these local dirt poor trash. Big John had told them they could rob the passengers and keep whatever they took. So they set to with a will, unearthing great rocks with their bare hands and tumbling them down.

The Renos were a different breed to their neighbours. They had had some schooling and manners knocked into them by their mother, a faded Kentucky beauty, who had had the misfortune to fall for their illiterate horse-breeder father, and never tired of telling her boys how superior they were to the common herd. She had had ambitions for them, but instead of doing good they had stuck together and gone solidly to the bad. Maybe the war had helped.

The brothers hunkered down over a small smoky fire and let the boys get on with building the barrier across the track. They brewed up coffee from fine-ground beans, and passed the steaming tin pail around to suck at as John drew with a stick in the leaves' mud the route of escape they would take.

'You figure they gonna have guards in the baggage car?' William asked, as he rolled a cigarette and watched their horses wildfeed.

'Who knows. There's allus some fool wants to act the hero,' Simeon drawled. 'What do we do, John, shoot to kill?'

'That depends,' he said, morosely. 'We don't want to kill nobody if it can be helped. We give 'em a chance to surrender first. We got plenty of boys along to take care of things. If there's guards there won't be more than two or three of 'em. What's that against fifteen guns?'

'Whee-hee!' Clinton whipped out his revolver, spun it on his finger and mock-fired across the heads of the

6

labouring boys. 'Bam! Bam!' He was the youngest of the Renos and had yet to grow any hair on his chin. Or, for that matter, grow up.

'Maybe we better cut the telegraph wire while we're at it,' Frank said, and took a pair of wire cutters from his pocket. 'Get up there, Clint. You're more nimble than me.'

While his brother monkeyed up the post, Big John went to take a look at the cinder bed of the railroad. There was a thirty-foot descent on one side. The sickle curve of the track was on a grade that would be hard work for any locomotive. It was getting dusk and the bare branches of the trees hung sinisterly low over the track. He consulted his brass pocket-watch. 'They should be leaving Seymour any minute now.'

An owl hooted, eerily, and, in spite of himself, John shivered. Like any operation, it was the waiting beforehand that was the worst. Nobody, as far as he knew, had tried stopping an express train on its track before. There had been a few derailed in the war but that was a different kettle of fish.

He lit a hurricane lamp and placed a red wool shirt over it. 'I'll go downtrack a hundred yards and wave this about. That should give 'em plenty of chance to stop.'

'We better go with you,' Frank said. 'The baggage car's usually down the back.'

'No, you take care of things this end. Put your gun to the head of the engineer. He ain't likely to argue. Keep an eye on these idjits. Me and the boys will take care of the express car.'

John turned and shouted to their helpers, who were still loading rocks across the rail. 'That's fine. You done well. Now, we don't want no killin' on this picnic. You all jest fire into the air, scare the living daylights outa the passengers and help yourselves to whatever they got. Come on, station yourselves along the track, either side. It's nearly time. Remember, no killing, not unless you have to.'

He strode away, his boots crunching on the gravel, followed by three of his brothers. They stood beneath the lonesome trees and waited. It had grown gloomily dark, the branches glistening with frost as a moon rose, the only sounds the shrill shriek of some critter being made supper of by a prowling predator.

'Clang! Clang!' The faint sound of the locomotive's warning bell drifted to them, followed by the 'shunt-shunt-shunt' of its labouring engine. Then they saw its cyclopean eye, the single beam of light coming around the curve in the track, the jetted out grey clouds of woodsmoke from its tall stack, and heard the sound of its rods churning the iron wheels of the engine, the clatter of the carriages and baggage car being hauled up the track.

'Here she comes,' Frank exclaimed, and drew his Smith and Wesson, spinning the cylinder, checking it was fully loaded, and tightening his grip on the ivory butt. 'Ready, boys?'

Down the track Big John began carefully brandishing the ruddy, glowing lamp from side to side. On and on the engine came as if the engineer was paying no attention to them, thundering louder and louder, as if he were going to charge into the ramp.

They jumped aside a split second before the cowcatcher reached them and heard the screech of brakes being applied, watched the shower of sparks, saw perplexed faces staring out of the passing windows as the locomotive shuddered to a halt not two feet from the barrier of tree and rocks. Big John Reno and his brothers had positioned themselves perfectly. There it was, right in front of them, the 'Adams Express Delivery Company' armoured car.

'They'll be making an unscheduled delivery tonight,' John roared, as all hell broke out along the line. The boys had set to firing their revolvers and longarms into the sky as if ammunition grew on the trees. Some went further, and smashed the glass of the windows in with the butts of their weapons, and yelled like Comanches as they clambered into the Pullman cars.

John Reno jerked one of his heavy Remingtons from his leather belt and studied the armoured Adams car. It was solidly built with one door and a small barred slit high up on it. He pulled himself up the steep steps and stood to one side as he shouted out, 'Open up!'

When there was no reply he shoved his Remington barrel through and fired four shots in fast succession. Black powder smoke drifted back from the hole but there was no cry of pain. Whoever was in there must have been keeping well out of range, too.

'Hot damn!' Simeon had climbed halfway up behind him. 'We should have brought gunpowder. How the hell we gonna git 'em to open up?'

Big John winked at him, and his bearded face creased into a grin. 'You guards in there, toss out your weapons.

You got three minutes to open up. Then we gonna blow this caboose to smithereens.'

There was no answer from within and John roared out, 'Boys, start piling them powder casks underneath.'

The seconds ticked by until the three minutes were almost through. 'OK, boys, light that fuse. Let's git outa here.'

A frightened face appeared at the window, an old man in a conductor's cap. 'Hold on, mister, I'm opening up. I don't care what these other two say.'

'Tell them other two to come out. We ain't gonna hurt 'em. They got no choice, 'less they want to join the angels up in the clouds. You need a match for that fuse, boys?'

Two Winchester carbines were thrust through the slit, the door was unbolted, and the conductor appeared, his hands in the air, followed by two surly men in civilian suits. 'OK,' one snarled. 'You win. We don't want no trouble.'

The guards were frisked, cuffed together with their own wrist manacles, and pushed to one side, and the Reno brothers climbed up and into the baggage wagon. There were parcels and mail bags, which they tore open, but they didn't appear to contain much of interest. Then they spotted a sturdy iron strong-box.

'Watch this,' Big John growled, putting the barrel of his revolver to the lock. He fired his two remaining slugs, shattering it. 'Jeesis Christ Awmighty,' he whispered, as he tipped back the lid. 'Jest look at that.'

The iron trunk was stashed to the lid with large-denomination brand-new greenback dollars, and sacks of gold coin. The four brothers stared at it as if they could hardly believe their eyes.

'What's going on?' Frank asked, as he pushed through the door to join them. He, too, stared at the cash. 'Good Lord! That railroad clerk sure weren't joking.'

'Boys,' John hooted. 'We're rich.

Rich as King Midas, whoever he was.'

'Come on. We can count it later. Let's get this stuff bagged up 'fore that other lot cotton on and want a share. Where are them gunny sacks?'

'How are the others doing? Any trouble?'

'They seem to be doing fine,' Frank said. 'There's some purty rich passengers in them Pullman cars. Ladies with jewels, men with gold watches. See, I got one for myself. Their guts ran to water when they saw the boys with their guns.'

'We've done it!' Big John slapped his brothers' shoulders and hands, yelling out loud. 'We've done it! We've robbed the darn Flyer. First ones to ever try!'

'Hang on,' Simeon said. 'We ain't finished yet. How about the safe?'

Their merriment slowly subsided as they stared at a great iron safe in a corner of the van. 'Go get that conductor up here,' Frank said.

'I cain't help you, boys. I only wish I could,' the little man squealed as he was dragged in by William, a knife at his throat. 'We don't have the key. You can search us. It was locked when we set out from Chicago and can only be opened when we reach Memphis.'

'Shee-it!' William hammered at the lock with his revolver butt. 'Why ain't we got no powder?'

They found big sledgehammers, crowbars, spades used on the railroad, and, for almost an hour, tried every way they could to get the iron door open, but it wouldn't budge.

'It ain't my fault, boys,' the conductor whined. 'It's a new idea. They don't trust us.'

'What's in there?' Frank demanded.

'Ooh, quite a bit. All sorts of valuables and bills of credit. I'm real sorry you're disappointed, believe me.'

'Yeah?' Big John glanced at him and gave the safe one last mighty swipe with his sledge. 'Bastard! Come on, let's go. It ain't no use. We got enough.'

'We sure have,' Clinton laughed. 'Five-way split. That's two thousand dollars each. Suits me. And how about these Winchesters? This year's model. Who gets these?'

'You keep your paws offen them,' Big John thundered. 'They go to me and Frank.'

Clinton, William and Simeon began to get busy filling sacks with cash and gold, giggling merrily as they carried them out to tie around their horses' necks.

In the passenger cars their dozen friends were similarly whooping it up, prodding their rifles into men, women and children, making them jump down beside the track, tearing their carpet-bags open, scattering their belongings. They showed no courtesy to the females, young or old, snatching baubles and bangles from their ears, throats and wrists. One of the hillbillies had made a fat old biddy hoist her skirts and was delving into her drawers searching for a hidden purse.

'They're happy enough,' Frank said. 'Let's leave 'em to it.'

16

'Yep. It's time we headed for Missouri.' John Reno hauled himself up onto his Morgan and pointed his second Remington at the conductor and two guards. 'I'd like to thank you gents for not giving us no trouble. You git back in that guard's van and lock yourselves in 'fore I count to ten. Or else.'

He laughed as they scrambled back for the safety of the van. 'You ever been had?'

'Yeah,' William yelled. 'We didn't have no darn gunpowder, you fools.'

'Thanks, anyway,' Big John rode along the line and shouted to the ragged men in their slouch hats. 'You boys split up and go your separate ways. We're going our'n. Maybe we'll see you again.'

The wall-eyed youth paused from going through an old gent's pockets. 'What did you find in the van?' he asked.

'Aw, nothing much,' Frank called. 'We couldn't get the damn safe open.

Just our luck. So long, boys.'

The oily-faced fireman and engineer were staring dolefully from their cab as the five brothers raced past on their thoroughbreds. Simeon fired a shot at the engine bell and it ricocheted off. 'Ca-Lang!' And they went galloping away down the track.

2

'Well, at least they didn't get their thieving hands on ten thousand dollars' worth of Adams Express bank-notes. That's some relief.' Allan Pinkerton spun the swivel armchair behind his desk and faced the two guards. 'But the headlines we're getting splattered across the journals from coast to coast could bankrupt us. And it's all due to you two bunglers.'

'What could we do, sir?' One of the railroad guards, Patrick Kilpatrick, shifted uncomfortably as he stood before his employer. 'There was a huge gang of 'em, all armed to the teeth. How did we know their threat was a bluff?'

He was a tall, broad-shouldered young man, his hair plastered down with grease, a bad dose of acne around his jaws. Tom Patterson, by his side, was an older, stockier man, who let him do the talking.

'I ought to fire you both for incompetence. I need men working for me who are prepared to put their lives on the line. God knows, I pay you enough.' Pinkerton, a fiery Glaswegian, had emigrated to the USA at the age of twenty-two and worked for eight years for the Chicago police force. In 1850 he established his own private detective agency in the city. 'I ought to kick your asses out of here.'

When they didn't reply, he added, 'Thank God I took the precaution not to let you have the key to the safe. Or the army of occupation in Memphis would never have got their pay. You two would have surrendered it like the ninnies you are.'

'Excellent idea of yours, sir,' Kilpatrick said. 'Unfortunately, all they needed to do was forge signatures of a bank president or chief cashier to use those unsigned Adams notes. A simple procedure for them.'

'Don't tell me something I'm well aware of, you sycophantic bastard,' Pinkerton snapped. 'Why 'for them'?'

'Because they've been involved in their home town with a counterfeiter called Pete McCartney issuing spurious bills. Strictly small-time, up until now.'

'Yes, and now they've created a precedent that every damn would-be criminal is going to imitate. It will be rob the railroads from hereon in. They'll all be jumping on the bandwagon.'

'We're pretty sure we know who they are,' Patterson ventured. 'The five Reno boys. They were brought up on a ranch outside Seymour. A murky history in the war. But anybody who knows how to keep from being cannon fodder must be a cut above his fellows.'

'An unpatriotic comment, but I see what you mean, Tom.' Pinkerton swivelled his chair back around and lit a pipe as he stared out of his window engraved with its large all-seeing eye

21

above the busy Chicago streets, and the motto 'We Never Sleep'. He, himself, had had a distinguished career in the war as intelligence officer to General McClellan, and, under the alias, 'Major E.H. Allan', organized a wide-reaching secret service for the Union army.

'What makes you think it's the Renos?'

'The sheriff down there picked up a couple of no-hopers who were trying to sell watches and jewellery, obviously property of the rail passengers. They put them on to others of the gang. The usual bunch of incompetents and social inadequates. They didn't need much leaning on to reveal that it was the Renos who set up the raid, principally Big John Reno.'

'So why haven't the Renos been arrested?' Pinkerton continued to stare out of the window as he puffed a cloud of acrid smoke from the deep-bowled pipe. 'Don't tell me they've done a disappearing act?'

'Skipped without much trace, sir,'

Kilpatrick eagerly volunteered. 'Although my own investigations led me to a young lady seamstress, Hetty Hancock. She admits to being the girlfriend of Frank Reno. I put some pressure on her and it seems Frank had promised marriage. They were going to take some of his father's Morgans out west to Missouri and start a stock ranch.'

'Morgans? What the hell are they?'

'All descended from one horse owned by a New Englander by the name of Justin Morgan in 1789,' Kilpatrick rattled out, eager to ingratiate himself with his employer. 'He got a bargain because the horse looked too light for draft work and too heavy for the saddle. But they're a magnificent breed, can outpull many a heavier horse and carry a rider fifty miles in a day with ease.'

'Yes, thank you for the lesson. So?'

'So,' Tom Patterson put in, 'we think the boys may be planning to put their stolen cash into starting their own ranch. It appears they have never got on well with their father. I went to visit him. He's a patriarch of the old school. He said they can go where the hell they like as far as he cares.'

'Their mother is a more cultivated lady, but obviously bullied by her husband. Both are disappointed their sons have deserted them, neglected their responsibilities at the ranch, and turned to crime. If you ask me the father gave them a hard time when they were kids.'

'So, good, we are beginning to build up a picture, are we not? A wild bunch, ruined by their war experiences, unable to settle to the peace, like so many who won't knuckle down, fond of Morgan horses, reasonably intelligent, could masquerade as horse dealers, and headed for Missouri. Have we any identification, descriptions, for the files?'

'I obtained a daguerreotype likeness of Frank Reno from the mother.' Patrick Kilpatrick opened his briefcase and produced it. 'Actually, I stole it from her dresser behind her back.'

'Good. You're using some initiative, at last.' Allan Pinkerton studied the likeness of Frank, with his wild black curls and jutting square of moustache and beard. 'He's not unlike that rebel guerrilla leader, Nathan Forrest, who did so much damage in Tennessee in the war. The same messianic air. Attired like a gentleman, too. Let's hope he isn't as wily as that old fox.'

Pinkerton was a great believer in building up extensive files on thousands of outlaws and fugitives, physical data, criminal records, modes of operation, even handwriting specimens. No detail was too small.

'Get all this on file,' he said. 'And get after them. Perhaps I can give the banks and railroad companies some hope that they will be apprehended before they strike again?'

'You think they will, sir?' Kilpatrick said. 'It seems to me this could be a one and only hit.'

'You think wrong.' Pinkerton sucked

dourly at his pipe. 'Don't delude yourselves.'

'At least nobody got hurt,' Tom Patterson put in. 'The folks I've spoken to down in Seymour seemed to think they weren't bad young fellows, just wild. Not psychopaths.'

'Don't kid yourself, Tom. It's only a matter of time before somebody gets killed. While you're out in Missouri it might be an idea to get in touch with Charlie Durango, one of our operatives, one of the best, in fact.'

'Where do we find him?'

'Here.' Pinkerton scribbled down an address, passed it across. 'You can't miss him, a real Westerner, tall, laconic, heavy grey moustache, wears his revolver tied down to his thigh with a rawhide thong for a fast draw, carries a Henry rifle. He's been after some stage robbers out there.'

As the two detectives prepared to leave the office, Pinkerton called, 'It might be an idea if you got out of those natty suits and derby hats and dressed to look the part.'

'We will, sir.'

'And don't forget' — Pinkerton pointed to his eye — 'We Never Sleep.'

★ ★ ★

The Renos rode their Morgans south, fording the River Ohio into Kentucky, and on south into war-torn Tennessee, making good time, easily out-distancing on their fine horses any possible pursuit. Snow had begun to fall, matting their coats in frost, and they camped out in the woods and brakes, a way of life they had become accustomed to in the war. They followed the loop of the great Tennessee River passing the ruined village of Shiloh where the grass was still stained dark with the blood of forty thousand men who slaughtered each other in two days. The population was still bitterly split, family against family, but few men cared to challenge five well-mounted and heavily armed desperadoes who cantered by.

Most of the countryside was in ruins, farm-houses destroyed, the population ragged and hungry. The states turned out more and more of their own currency on their printing presses, which was practically worthless. And the National Bank tried to stabilize Federal green-backs by taxing State currency out of existence.

'The whole country's in a mess,' Big John growled, as they sat around their camp fire one dark night. 'The ordinary man don't have a chance. We might be robbers but we're no worse than that gang of thieves in Washington led by President Grant.'

They reached Memphis City on the bank of the wide Mississippi where there was a heavy army presence and rebuilding going on. The collaborators during the war, the carpetbaggers who had flooded in afterwards, the profiteers, lived there in high style. Women in fine dresses, with army officers in coach-and-four on their way to shindigs and balls, mingled with freed uppity blacks and soldiers crowding the sidewalks. Not everybody was poor. And with greenbacks and gold aplenty the Reno boys joined in the free-and-easy spending in the saloons, gambling halls and on the riverbanks. Unfortunately, they were no match for the professional cardsharps, or, for that matter, the nimble-fingered whores, whites and mulattos. Soon most of their money was frittered away.

'Boys, it's been good fun, wine, women and whiskey galore, but we gotta get outa here,' Frank said, troubled by the way their cash was disappearing. He missed Hetty, who had begged him to take her along with them, and he had promised to send for her when they found themselves a piece of land in Missouri. Ten thousand dollars had seemed like a fortune, but it was dripping away like water through a colander. He persuaded his brothers to saddle up, load their horses onto a ferryboat, and cross the Big River.

John, too, was troubled. It was all right for his younger brothers to go gallivanting around, but he had always been the more solemn and sober one. He had been let down by a woman when he was younger and had taken against the 'flighty female gender', as he saw them. He was superstitious, moody, believed strongly in ghosts and the 'Other Life', and was prone to staring at the moon. He studied obscure passages of the Bible and was deeply cynical about the human race which he saw as hell-bent upon self-destruction. He, too, agreed it was time to put their shoulders to the plough.

It was not going to be as easy as they thought. Winter was fast setting in, and harsh blizzards swept the countryside. They bought a property near a town called Davies. But it was ramshackle. Rain leaked through the roof, and the fences were badly in need of repair. They had come unprepared. Their father had refused to provide them with brood Morgan mares, which they believed to be due to them. They could breed half-Morgans, but the horses in these parts were runty stock hardly worth five dollars a head. It all took time and a lot of enterprise even to build-up a half-successful ranch. And, even if they did, wasn't there a chance that some nosy US marshal might arrive with arrest warrants and all the effort would be wasted?

The land was flat and ugly, what few neighbours there were were suspicious and unfriendly. Christmas passed drearily. They sat out the harsh months of January, February and March, playing desultory poker for pennies. It was like suffering from cabin fever. They could escape to the saloon at Davies, but what was there to do there? They only had to come back. For the past six years of the war and its aftermath they had grown used to a fast, exciting life. Big John and Frank really wanted to go straight, settle down, but it was hard.

'Hell,' Clinton drawled one day as

they huddled around the pot-bellied stove, the rain lashed down and the shutters shook. 'There ain't nuthin' to do here 'cept fish or fuck and nobody to fuck with.'

'You could allus go find a cow,' Simeon said.

They all laughed, but in their hearts agreed. Ploughing, sowing, scything, tending cattle and horses from dawn to dusk, out in the cold and mud, what life was that? They had suffered it under their father's harsh rod. None of them, to tell the truth, was keen on hard work.

'Boys,' John said, 'I think its time we recouped our fortunes.' He had been away riding alone for days and dried himself at the stove. 'I been taking a look at the Davies county treasury. I reckon we could just ride in there and help ourselves. It's ripe for plucking.'

'What we gonna do then?' Clinton asked. 'Head on into Indian territory? We won't be able to hang around here.'

'No, I figure it's time to head home,' Frank said. 'I've a hankering to see Hetty.'

Yes, they all agreed. They missed their old haunts. They began, more cheerfully, to soap their saddles, oil their carbines. In the morning they packed their bedrolls, hauled on boots, hats and rainproofs, saddled up and, carbines under their arms headed into Davies. It had to be. All, or nothing.

'Boys, loosen up,' Simeon sang out as they rode and the sun glimmered through murky clouds. 'I can smell spring in the air.' /

'And cash, too,' Clinton laughed.

It was an unimposing town, more a collection of loose-strung shanties and wooden false-fronts, a grain silo and stores set down on the wide plain. But it was the administrative centre of the county, with its own brick-built council hall, sheriff's office, and treasury hall combined. From here government loans were granted to homesteaders, and payments made to railroaders pushing the track west towards Indian territory.

'Yep,' Big John muttered, as they ambled their Morgans down the wide main street. 'I figure they must have a coupla thousand for expenses in that building. It'll see us through.'

Nobody paid them much heed, the five young men in slickers and greatcoats, wide-brimmed hats, on their fiery stallions, none of which, however, weighed more than twelve hundred pounds and contained a deceptive power. Not that there were many folk to pay them heed, a few gossiping homesteaders' wives on their wagons come to do some shopping, some idlers seeking warmth in the saloon and barbershop. The only sound was the drip of icicles melting as the thaw set in, the clang of the blacksmith's hammer on anvil as he watched them go by.

They dismounted, all but William, who they left to hold the horses and keep a watch out. John, Frank, Simeon and Clinton eyed each other, grimly, levered slugs into their carbines, and swung forward on their heavy boots towards the treasury doors. Frank looked at his stolen gold watch. It was 10 a.m.

3

Tom Patterson clambered stiffly from his ornery mustang as it turned its head and tried to bite him. 'Git out of it, you mangy piece of dogfood,' he growled, dragging the mustang over to the hitching rail. 'This brute just don't like me. Why did I ever leave Chicago?'

'You got to show him who's boss.' Kilpatrick jumped down from his own mount, tied it alongside, and stepped up to the sidewalk of the Grotto Saloon, Independence, Missouri. 'This is one bustling town.'

The city was the gathering point for settlers joining trains of covered wagons preparing to head out on the long trek west through hostile Indians, across prairies and mountains, towards the promised lands of California and Oregon. Kilpatrick watched several of these oxen-drawn wagons ploughing through the deep mud of the main street, their occupants cursing and shouting. They had bought their supplies from the numerous emporiums, gunshops and stores and it was 'Californee-yay, or bust!'

'This the place?' Patterson asked.

In his bearhide coat, battered hat and heavy boots, he looked more like a badman than a lawman, and had grown a beard against the bitter cold as they combed through Missouri these past months. They had started in the southern Ozarks and West Plain, pushed up through to Springfield onto the Missouri River and Jefferson City, and here they were on the north-west border without a scent of the Reno boys.

'That's what it says in the telegraph.' Kilpatrick towered over him, his suit protected by hat, boots and rain slicker from the weather. He hoped he looked equally the Westerner, but he insisted on wearing a smart celluloid collar and tie, and shaving, so his jaws were a mess of bloody nicked zits. 'Let's take a look.'

When they pushed through the wooden door the noise and aroma coming from a mass of unwashed, hairy muleskinners, homesteaders, snakeoil salesmen, and a few bedraggled *filles de joie,* nearly knocked them out. A piano tinkled in the background as they peered through the canopy of tobacco smoke.

'Maybe that's him?' Kilpatrick nodded across at a long-legged galoot sprawled at a table in the corner, his back to the wall. His hair and thick moustache were white, and his hard-chiselled face the colour of mahogany. He wore a grey tweed suit and big spotted bandanna. A long-barrelled Paterson was pig-stringed to his thigh. A big old Henry rifle was leaned by his side and he had a hand on a bottle of rye whiskey.

'That's our man.' The stocky Patterson elbowed his way across through the press, and faced the *hombre*. 'Howdy,' he said.

'Who the hell are you?' The stranger, who might well have been taken for some gun-slinger, had an aggressive whiskey growl to his tone. 'You're blocking my light.'

Patterson touched his right eye and winked. 'We ain't had no sleep for days. Hope we ain't kept you?'.

They were the rather elementary code words and Charlie Durango grinned. 'You boys want a taste of my whiskey? Or you can help yourself to beaver stew from that big pot on the stove, though Hell knows how many weeks it's been brewing.'

'It'll do,' Patterson grunted, as he pulled off his heavy fur coat, tossed it onto the floor. 'Get a coupla bowls of it, Pat.'

Durango offered him the bottle and he grabbed it by the neck, took a couple of good pulls and sighed, rubbing his hands. 'That's better. I'm sick of this damn wild goose chase.'

He filled the Westerner in on what little information he had on the Renos as Kilpatrick brought them steaming hot wooden bowls of stew, which was free to all who imibed the saloon's alcohol. 'We've combed through this territory but we ain't seen hide or hair of 'em.' He wiped a tear from his nose as he gulped the gamey food down. 'This is good. I don't know why the boss wants us to keep on after 'em. They could be anywhere. Probably in California by now.'

'He sees it as personal,' Kilpatrick said. 'They were the first ones to rob us.'

'Yeah, well, it's personal with me, but not that personal. There's no hope in hell of getting the cash back.'

Durango refilled his tumbler with what was left in the bottle. 'You better buy another of these. I been waiting for you a week. I'm getting used to it. I coulda stayed at Fort Smith and seen my boys hanged, but Pinkerton's telegraph said this was urgent.'

'What boys?'

'Aw, coupla 'breed rustlers and stage robbers been causing mayhem in the Nations. I had to bring 'em in.'

'Hmm?' Patterson eyed him. He had heard he was from Wyoming, had a reputation as a no-nonsense crack shot. 'What you use that for?' he asked, wagging his spoon at the Henry. 'Shooting buffalo?'

'Sometimes,' Durango grinned. 'Sometimes men. It don't leave much of their heads.'

'Yeah?' Pinkerton had told him he had met Charlie Durango during the war when he worked as a scout for the Union troops who took Missouri, infiltrating Confederate lines to spy on their positions. He had been an Indian fighter, a Pony Express rider, and a cattle drover. His age was anybody's guess. His white hair was deceptive. Maybe that was the fault of the scrapes he had been in, or the whiskey. 'Bit early to be drinking, isn't it?' He looked

41

up at a big clock on the wall. It was exactly 10 a.m.

'Yeah?' Durango spat away the cork of a fresh bottle. 'Maybe it is. Maybe it ain't.'

★ ★ ★

The clerks seated on stools behind the counter of Davies City treasurer's office looked up, quill pens poised, stunned by the sight of the four desperadoes, the carbines levelled at them.

'Don't nobody make a sound,' Big John said, in a husky growl. 'Let's do this nice 'n' easy, shall we?'

They had already surprised the town sheriff in a similar way, and he was currently gagged, hand-cuffed and locked in his own cell. There were only three people being attended to in the cashier's department.

One of them in front of him, a farmer, he relieved of his revolver, and tucked it in his own pocket. He turned his Winchester on another man, who had a shotgun half-raised. What was he, the treasury guard? 'I wouldn't do that, mister.'

'If he does, she gets it.' Clinton had put a brawny arm around the neck of a young woman standing at the grille, and dragged her back into him. He had his carbine barrel to her temple. 'It would be a pity to blow away such a purty face.' He grinned, and licked his tongue up her cheek, staring at the guard.

'Same goes for anybody makes a false move,' Simeon shouted, as he pointed his carbine through the protective bars above the counter. 'Somebody better open up this gate.'

'What's it to be?' John coaxed the guard. 'You just break that shotgun, take out the shells, and lay it down on the floor nice 'n' easy. OK? Then nobody gets hurt.'

'Otherwise,' Frank put in, 'we could end up killin' the whole damn lot of you. We don't want to do that, do we?'

The guard hesitated, and slowly did as he was bid, laying the shotgun down, kicking it across, and backing away against the wall. 'Watch him, Simeon. If he makes a move, bop him.' Big John turned his attention to the cashiers. 'Who's in charge? Whoever it is is going to let us through and open up that safe.'

No one spoke for moments although all eyes turned to a stoop-shouldered man in a green eye-shade.

'Very well,' he said, pulling out a ring of keys. 'I see I have no choice. Don't do anything foolish, boys. Please don't hurt us. We've got wives and families.'

'Get the vault open,' Frank said, as he let them through the gate at the side of the counter. 'That's all you got to do.'

'You want us to take her hostage?' Clinton called, gripping hold of the woman's breasts. 'We could do with her. I ain't had a roll in the hay in months. How you fancy that, honey?'

The chief cashier shrugged, hopelessly, and unlocked a huge combination wall safe. 'Don't let him take her,' he said. 'Just help yourselves and go.'

'Gee!' John looked inside at the shelves stacked with treasury notes. 'Don't mind if we do. Who's got that gunny sack?'

He and Frank carefully removed the wads of dollars, as Clinton giggled and whispered obscene words into the young woman's ear. Simeon kept the others covered.

'How much is there in here?' Frank asked the chief cashier as he cleared the shelves.

'I do believe there's twenty-two thousand and sixty-five dollars, sir.'

'Good.' Frank tucked a five-dollar note in his pocket. 'Buy yourself a cigar. You've been very helpful.'

'Oh, I'm not allowed to do that, sir.'

But Frank and John weren't listening. They were walking briskly away out of the building, Simeon backing after them, Clinton dragging the woman to the door, then hurling her away, and making a run for it.

'It's crazy,' Frank grinned, as they leapt onto their horses. 'It's like taking candy from a baby.'

They touched spurs to their eager Morgans and went like a rocket out of town, speeding away in a beeline east across the snowy plain.

4

The Renos' Morgans outpaced any posse that might be sent after them. After they crossed the Big River, they put their stallions into the goods vans of the same railroad company they had robbed, The Ohio and Missouri, and travelled back to Seymour in style. In the Pullman cars there were comfortable sleeping berths, velvet drapes and fine furniture, exotic six-course menus, and champagne on call, for those who could afford it (others went second class). The brothers, with five thousand dollars each in their wallets, wanted nothing but the best.

Frank had sent a telegraph to Hetty, who had notified various of their acquaintances, so that when they rolled into Seymour they were greeted like conquering heroes by a crowd of riff-raff, the town band pumping out martial airs. 'We're back,' John roared, raising his fist. 'And this time we're gonna stay.'

The mayor, storekeeper Hyram J. Jones, and a small group of other solid citizens, including Major Ike McLaury, a former professional soldier, watched, perplexed. Led by the major they stormed across to the office of the town sheriff, Abe Wappenshaw. 'What are you going to do about this?' Jones demanded. 'Those men should be apprehended.'

'It ain't nuthin' to do with me,' Wappenshaw whined, as he looked nervously up at them from his desk. 'Arresting 'em's railroad business. They ain't broken any town ordinances far as I see. Anyhow, there's five of them and they're crack shots. Any of you going to help me?'

No sooner had the disgruntled townspeople gone than John Reno himself pushed into the sheriff's office. He was big of girth, and his black eyes were menacing. He threw back his

48

caped greatcoat to reveal the brace of Remington revolvers in his belt. 'Howdy, Abe,' he said. 'You got anything you want to say to me?'

Wappenshaw twiddled his thumbs on the desktop. 'Hello, John. No, I don't have nothing to say. You keep your brothers in line, that's fine by me. I don't want no trouble.'

'Good to hear it.' John kicked the door shut behind him, and took a roll of notes from his vest pocket. He peeled off a fifty dollar, slapped it down on the desk. 'There's one like that every week. You just keep your nose out of our affairs.'

Sheriff Wappenshaw stared at the note, watched Reno amble out to a gang of men waiting. Through the window he saw them heading towards the town saloon, the Red Garter. He picked up the fifty and gave a low whistle as he tucked it in his pocket. 'This sure is a turn-up,' he muttered. 'I ain't no gunslinger. What am I supposed to do?'

Over in the Garter there was celebration as John Reno ordered drinks on the house for everyone. 'We're taking over this town,' he shouted. 'And we're gonna run it the way we choose. No damn town council gonna tell us what to do. Any you boys want to put your name down on my payroll? I'm looking for forty good men. Men who know how to use a gun and are looking for adventure. But, I warn you, we don't want no lowdown itchy-fingered murderers. We Renos are God-fearing. We haven't killed anybody yet and we don't want to. That is our proud boast. The only way we will use our guns is in self-defence.'

There was a mighty cheer from the men packed in the saloon, who clamoured to have their glasses filled and assure the Renos of their loyalty. Many of them were cousins, or distant blood relatives, former boyhood friends, or soldiers who had ridden alongside them in the war. Most were disillusioned with the peace, the politicians, the economic chaos, and just life in general. It was time to show the world they weren't to be trifled with.

'Of course,' Frank yelled. 'We might have a hell of a lot of defending to do. You boys better be ready to see lead fly. We ain't gonna allow nobody in this town we don't want here.'

He had his arm around Hetty, protecting her from the crush, and she smiled up at him, anxiously. 'Are you sure you're doing the right thing, Frank? Won't they send the military in after you?'

'The military ain't interested in us. They got too much to attend to, the Indian wars, occupying the South. They leave civil matters to town courts. The only ones to come after us are the railroad companies, or maybe some Missouri hick marshal. That's why we got to be ready for 'em.'

Hetty was slim-waisted and full-chested in an ankle-length dress of green velvet she had sewn herself. It was pinned modestly at the throat by an ivory cameo. She was wearing a large velvet hat from beneath which her dark brown eyes peered up at him. 'What went wrong in Missouri, Frank?'

'Aw, it's a long story. Here, have a drop of this.' He put his thumbs to a champagne cork and popped it. 'I got it on the train. Frenchy stuff. Gives you a real buzz. Maybe I'll bring the other bottle round to your place tonight.'

'Maybe.' Hetty was nervous of him. He seemed so rough and rowdy among the noisy men. Not as she remembered him. A fiddle had started scraping, and some disreputable 'poor trash' girls had started dancing and singing. This was not the sort of place she would normally frequent. She had her reputation to think of. The bubbles of the champagne were getting up her nose, but it was sweet, pleasant, yes, heady. She squeezed Frank's waist to get his attention. 'You said you were going to find us a place, somewhere we could settle down.'

'I've told ya, Hetty, it didn't work out. Don't worry, we'll find ourselves a little ranch. But first,' he grinned, 'we're gonna need more cash. Here, have another drop. Get you in the mood.'

'You're not planning on doing any more robberies, are you, Frank? You told me just the once. We'd go away. We'd be set for life.'

'So, we will be, Hetty. We'll have the finest, dandiest place you ever dreamed of. We done it wrong last time. I'm gonna buy up fifty Morgan stallions and mares and take 'em out far West. Come on, sweetheart, lighten up. Ain't you pleased to see me?'

'Sure I am, Frank,' she said, fluttering her lips against his cheek. 'But this place ain't for me. I'll go shut up shop. Stoke up the fire. You come along when you want to, but don't leave it too late.'

'Sure thing, Hetty. We got a lot of catching up to do. Yee-hoo!' He whirled her around, kicking his heels, waltzing her to the door. 'You be on your way. I'll be around in a half-hour or so.'

He lurched back to the bar and slapped Simeon and William on their backs, calling for their glasses to be refilled. 'It sure is good to be home, ain't it, boys?'

★ ★ ★

The Renos didn't intend any harm to the towns-people of Seymour. Nor to any ordinary folks. Just as long as they toed the line and didn't interfere with them. They turned the saloon and the railroad depot into their headquarters. Hank Diprose was still the chief railroad clerk there and looked a tad disgruntled until Big John slapped a wad of five hundred dollars down in front of him. 'Didn't have time to give you this 'fore we left town. I'm a man of my word. Any more information you can get us of a similar nature you'll get your cut, Hank. We're mighty obliged to you.'

He had recruited his gang of followers at ten dollars a week, with promise of a bonus when they 'hit'. They were men like his cousins, Wilk and Trick Reno, Jesse Thompson, Billy Biggers, Miles Ogle, Charlie Spencer, Albert Perkins and Fee Johnson. These weren't God-fearing men, in fact, remarkably wild and dissolute at times. But he figured he could keep them in line.

Big John had not given credence to the brutishness of men's nature, especially ignorant, wild, backwoodsmen of their ilk. No sooner had they been given power over the people of the small town than that power went to their heads. They swaggered about the sidewalks, longarms in their hands, making honest folk step aside. Jesse Thompson and his cronies lurched into Mayor Jones' emporium, helping themselves to cigars, bulls' eyes, biscuits, bottles of hooch, blankets, grinning and fooling about, pushing other customers aside.

'OK, boys,' Jones said, totting up the purchases. 'That'll be 265 dollars. How you going to pay for this?'

'Put it on the bill,' Jesse growled, chawing on a cigar.

'What bill?'

'The bill for protecting this town, fat ass. An' while we're at it I'll take one of them saddles. The cinch on mine's plumb wore out.'

'Oh, no you won't,' Jones protested.

'Oh, yes, we will.' Jesse laughed as he grabbed his face and shoved him toppling back to land in a barrel of hickory nuts. The others guffawed as they stomped out, as if at some great joke.

The Renos had ridden out to visit their parents' ranch, but they got no great welcome. 'You're no sons of mine.' Their father stood on the porch brandishing a shotgun, refusing to let them pass. 'You've dragged our name in the mud. Get off my land. I want no truck with thieves.'

'We ain't thieves, Pa,' Clinton protested. 'We've only taken from them who can afford it, the banks, the railroad.'

'You're spineless scum, the lot of you,' the old man ranted. 'You're all scared of honest work. What makes you think you can ride roughshod over everyone else?'

'Don't be so hard, Jim,' their mother pleaded. 'At least, let Clinton stay. He's only a boy. He don't belong with them.'

'Come on,' Frank shouted, swinging his thoroughbred's head around. 'Let's go. We know where we ain't wanted.'

'So long, Ma,' Clinton shouted. 'Don't you worry. We'll be OK.'

Back in town the Renos sat morosely in the saloon, while their men skulked like wolves, waiting for orders, waiting for the day they were going to be let loose. They looked to the Renos to lead them, to find them riches and notoriety.

Mayor Jones and Doc Dooley led a contingent of tradesmen to remonstrate with Big John Reno about the depredations of his men, their unruly, thieving behaviour.

'Judge not lest ye be judged,' John said, raising his Bible, glowering at them. 'You've skinned us for long enough. Now it's our turn. Anyhow, the boys don't mean no harm. It's just high spirits.' The traders trooped out of the saloon, red-faced and indignant, as Miles Ogle stuck out a boot and tripped gunshop-owner, Harry Henshaw. The boys thought that hilarious, and howled with laughter as they followed the deputation out, and sent bullets flying about their heads and feet, scattering them back to their premises.

'We gotta do something,' Mayor Jones gasped to the white-haired old doctor, as he slammed the shutters of his emporium. 'We can't go on like this. This is total lawlessness.'

'Why,' the doctor asked, 'don't the

58

sheriff do something?'

'Because he ain't got the guts,' Jones said. 'It looks like it's down to us if we're ever to get a decent community back together again.'

5

'Boys, I'll go on into Seymour, see what's goin' on,' Charlie Durango drawled. 'It ain't no use you comin' in with me. They'd recognize you.'

The two Pinkerton men eyed each other, uneasily. They had drawn in their horses in the woods on the edge of town, unsure what tactics to use now they had finally caught up with the Renos. 'I'm not so sure that's a good idea,' Tom Patterson said. 'What the hell you gonna do on your own?'

Durango tugged at his white moustache and tipped his tall Capper and Capper over his eyes, spurring his horse away. 'I'll get the drop on them, somehow, bring one or all of them varmints out.'

'He's nothing if not confident,' Kilpatrick grinned.

Durango wheeled his grey back,

pulled the big Henry rifle from the saddle boot, and handed it across. 'Maybe you better look after this. Just in case. I don't want to lose it like you did them Winchesters of your'n. It's an old friend. Wait for me here, boys. I'll try not to be too long.'

Patterson watched him go and winced as he held the Henry. The loss of their hundred-dollar Winchester carbines to the Renos still rankled. They had been brought out the previous year, '66, a greatly improved version of the Henry, a less complicated firing mechanism, with shiny brass butt plate and frame. The short-barrelled carbine carried a dozen .44 calibre rimfire cartridges of twenty-eight grains. Admittedly, it was not as powerful as the Henry, but an ideal saddle gun. They had been unable to purchase replacements at short notice and had to make do with seven-shot Spencers.

'Old Ben Henry certainly knows a thing or two about fire-arms.' Patterson squinted along the sights and levered a slug into the rifle chamber from the tubular magazine beneath the barrel, which cocked the rifle ready for firing. Henry was superintendent at the Winchester firm.

'Beats me why the army was never interested in buying 'em,' Kilpatrick replied, as he jumped down and tethered his mustang to a branch.

'Too heavy, I guess, but damnably accurate in the right hands.' Patterson laid the rifle aside, hugging his bear fur around him, preparing for a long wait. 'Anyway them old grannies in the War Office don't know nuthin'. We better not light a fire. Don't want to give our position away.'

'Looks like we got cold water and hard tack for supper,' Kilpatrick sighed. 'What a life!'

* * *

Hetty Hancock was hanging out her washing in the garden of her cottage on the edge of town. She was a tad despondent due to her relationship with Frank Reno, if relationship it could be called. All his fine promises, and nothing had changed. In fact, things had just gotten worse. That first night still rankled. He had arrived at the cottage hours after she had left him, disgracefully drunk, by which time the nice meal she had prepared in celebration of his homecoming was burned and ruined. Hetty was a girl who believed in the niceties of life. She liked to be wooed. Instead Frank had thrust her onto the bed, had his way with her, in spite of her protestations. It made her feel as cheap as some two-bit whore. And since then things hadn't improved. He spent most of his time in the Red Garter saloon and only came to see her when he was either hungry or randy.

Hetty pegged a pair of drawers up on the line. It wasn't right, she thought, the way he treated her, like some concubine. Would he or wouldn't he marry her? A girl needed to know, especially if there was every possibility she might become pregnant by him. Hetty was an independent young lady, but she had no wish to be an unmarried mother. 'Aw, heck,' she said to herself. 'He ain't never going to go straight. What's the point of me kiddin' myself?'

It rankled, too, the way the Reno gang had practically taken over the town, rampaging around like hooligans. Because of her association with Frank it had got to the point where decent folk were cutting her in the street, not coming into her dress shop any more. In fact, due to lack of trade, she had closed up early that day and come home to get on with some chores.

Hetty was about to take her empty clothes basket in when she spied a stranger riding along the trail into town. He was a lanky fellow in a tall hat, and rough, homespun grey suit. The high horn of a Denver saddle, stuck up between his legs, denoted that he was not from these parts. He was deeply suntanned, and tugged at the droopy corners of a thick white moustache. 'Howdy, ma'am,' he drawled, touching his hat as he reined in by the garden gate. 'Maybe you could tell me where I could find the Renos?'

'I'm miss, not ma'am.' Hetty held the basket to her tummy, scowling up at him. 'The Renos? What do you want with them?'

He gave a flicker of a smile, a curdle of humour in his stone-grey eyes. 'You mighty direct, aincha?'

'Well, it's none of my business, I'm sure. You'll no doubt find them in the saloon, guzzling bourbon and pickling their brains. Or at the rail depot.'

'I was in the vicinity and I heard tell they were looking for men who can handle a gun.' He patted the Texas Paterson tied to his thigh. 'I'm low on funds so I'm thinking of volunteering.'

'Oh, so you're a gunslinger. How nice to know. If I were you, mister, I'd turn right round and go look to use your gun some other place. This town don't need you.' Hetty's dark eyes burned fiercely as she looked up at him, and she pushed her hair from her brow. 'We've got enough troublemakers here. There used to be a time when we could hold our heads up and say we'd got a town worth living in.'

'Sorry to hear you feel like that, miss. A man's got to do what a man's got to do.' Durango took a leather-covered drinking flask from his pocket and took a nip. 'One thing about this country — you sure know how to make good bourbon.'

'So, another whiskey-breath, too.'

'It's a failing of mine, I must admit,' Durango said, 'but one that don't do no harm, except perhaps to my kidneys.'

'It's the devil's poison. It creates nothing but mischief.'

'Gee, you're as fierce as a li'l bantam hen,' Charlie grinned. 'What I ever done to you?'

'Your kind ain't welcomed by decent

folks and it's best you know it.'

Hetty turned to go back into her cottage, but the stranger sat his horse by the white picket fence and chuckled. 'It sure is nice to know you're a single lady, miss. Purty chickadee like you. Here's one sinner appreciates a gal who knows what's right, even if she don't approve of me. How about if I called on you one day, when my business in this town is done, and asked you to step out with me?'

Hetty stood in her porch and looked back at him. There was something amusing about the stranger, maybe his nerve, his way of talking. And, in spite of what he was, she hadn't had a man tell her she was pretty in a long time. Most didn't dare. She was regarded as Frank Reno's property.

'Thank you,' she said, smiling in spite of herself — his grin was sort of infectious — 'but I have a fiancé. It would be advisable if you didn't bother me. Frank has a very short fuse.'

'Frank?' Durango held the reins of

his big, grey-mottled horse high, and it stirred restlessly. 'That sounds familiar.' He let the horse go on its way.

Hetty watched him go. He had a cheek. He was old enough to be her father. That white hair and moustache. But there was something that intrigued her about the rider. 'No, he's just some damn no-good,' she said, and shut the door.

* * *

Charlie Durango slid from the grey and looked about him. The usual kind of small town, a wide, muddy main street lined on both sides with stores of various kinds, sheriff's office, rail depot, the one saloon. The Red Garter. Fancy name. He caught sight of a couple of men posted up on rooftops, rifles in their hands. Another sour-faced thug was sat in a rocking-chair outside the saloon, a shotgun across his knees. This might prove harder than he thought. And there was something in the air, a tension, a lack of small-town easygoing familiarity, women standing gossiping, that kind of thing. And children had been kept off the street. An air of menace, in fact.

He climbed the sidewalk and pushed through the bat-wing doors, his jingle-bob spurs rattling as he swung across the wooden floor to the bar. Men at tables playing cards turned to regard him, balefully. Best to try to ingratiate himself and wait his chance. 'Howdy,' he said to the 'keep. 'Make it a bourbon. And a beer chaser. I come a long way.'

The barkeep thumped a bottle of Kentucky bourbon on the bar and went to fill a glass. He sent the frothy beer sliding along the bartop to Durango's hand. Charley put a boot on the brass bar rail and took a good bite of the bourbon. 'Nice town you got here,' he said, to no-one in particular. 'I'm looking for a man called Big John Reno.'

The saloon fell silent for moments.

'He ain't here,' a youth with a wall-eye sneered. 'What you want with him?'

'Heard tell he was paying ten dollars a week. I could use that sort of money for a while.'

'Why, you broke or something?' The wall-eyed Abel Finnegan was leaning on the bar some distance away, in filthy undervest and pants held up by string. He had a revolver shoved in the top of one of his heavy boots, and probably a knife in the other. His gingery hair was lank and long. 'What you doin' in these parts?'

'Waal, seein' as you look like gutter trash I guess I can tell you,' Charlie drawled. 'We did a li'l raid in Liberty, Missouri, but it kinda went wrong. Men got killed. Reward posters out on a dozen of us. So I decided it might be more healthy this side of the river.'

'Liberty?' Abel echoed. 'But that was the James boys.'

'That's right. And it was me did the killin', so they ain't so friendly disposed to me. I'm riding alone.'

'Well, you better just ride on, friend,' a louder voice broke in, that of Big John, who was standing on the landing outside his room, looking down. 'I don't hire no itchy-fingered killers. I abide by the tenth commandment.'

'The feller pulled a gun so I had to plant him,' Charlie said. 'There's allus one. Normally I'm a follower of the commandments, myself, 'cept the one 'bout adultery.'

This brought forth a limp laugh from the assembled men, which was quelled as Big John came down the staircase, his bearded face severe. 'And just who else was on this little expedition of your'n in Missouri?'

Durango began to spiel out the names of the men in the raid. He ought to know. He had been after them for a year now. And he told how it had been done, and more of his 'history'.

'Hmm,' Big John mused. 'Sounds like a mighty impressive history. So, you decided you'd come and join us, huh?'

71

'You're famous,' Charlie grinned. 'I like your style. You go for the big prize, nice and clean, no unnecessary gunplay.'

'So, you're changing your mind now? Boasting about killin' some cashier when you came in. Now you say you don't like to do that sort of thing. Thought you could impress us, huh? Mister, how do we know you ain't some kind of marshal?'

Charlie shrugged, took a swig of his beer, wiped the back of his hand across his mouth, and turned to size up Big John. 'I guess you jest have to trust me, thass'all.'

'Mister, I don't trust nobody.'

The Westerner straightened up, tense as a man in a lion's den, and his right hand made a faint movement towards the butt of his Paterson. 'I'm offering you my services, what more can I say?'

'Mister, we don't need them.'

As Durango's hand moved nearer his revolver, every man in the room came up with a carbine or handgun, their deathly holes encircling him. 'Waal,' he grinned, letting the long-barrelled revolver slip back into the holster. 'You boys sure ain't friendly. Guess I'll just be moseying on.'

Big John nodded to Abel who had manoeuvred around behind Durango. Abel cracked the butt of his Colt Navy on the back of the lawman's neck, felling him. He stooped to take his gun, go through his pockets. 'Nuthin' much 'cept 'bout fifty dollars,' Abel said, quickly pocketing it.

'So much for the fast gunslinger,' Frank laughed, as he, too, came down the staircase, a carbine ready in his hands. 'Well done, John. You reckon he's telling the truth?'

Durango was groaning, trying to get to his feet. John Reno put his boot in his gut, hard. And kicked him again, 'Come on, mister. Let's have it for real now. Who are you?'

'Git lost,' Charlie mumbled, and again climbed to his knees. 'I told you who I was.'

Frank Reno cracked his carbine across his jaw, dislodging a tooth, drawing blood. 'You're a liar, that's what you are. We don't like strangers in this town, especially strangers from Missouri. OK, boys, work him over. Make him talk.'

'It'll be a pleasure,' Abel grinned, hauling Durango up by his bandanna and slapping his face. 'Come on, mister. You and me gonna have a little talk. Who you really working for?'

'Stick some matches under his nails,' one of the watching men laughed. 'That'll make him talk.'

However, Charlie Durango was as tough as rawhide, a tougher man than they had bargained for. Whatever they did to him over the next half-hour, which was not very pleasant, at least, for him, he only growled, 'Git lost.'

'That's enough,' Big John boomed. 'This is gettin' monotonous. And it's puttin' me off my food. I don't want him killed. I ain't gonna hang for some Missouri lawman or saddle tramp. Tie him on his hoss. Send him back where he come from. Might serve as a warning to whoever he's with.'

They dragged the semi-conscious Durango out, threw him across the grey, tied him by his wrists and ankles below the beast's belly, and whooping and hollering, they whacked its flanks and sent it skittering down the main street. A few parting shots around its hooves and it went galloping away back along the trail the way it had come.

Hetty had been alarmed by the commotion. She came to her garden gate and saw the bloodstained stranger tossing like a sack of potatoes across the saddle as the wild-eyed grey streaked by. 'Oh, my God,' she whispered. 'What have they done to him?'

★ ★ ★

Tom Patterson heard the thudding of a horse's hooves coming fast along the trail. He ran to take a look and saw the grey galloping hell for leather towards him, kicking up his heels, the bit between his teeth, and something — someone? — slung across his saddle. He pulled off his bearskin coat and stood his ground, flapping it in the horse's face. The grey skidded to a halt and reared up, flailing his hooves, whinnying and snorting, possibly thinking it was a real grizzly. Tom took the opportunity to grab at his reins and tried to calm him.

'Whoa, boy. Steady now.'

'It's Durango,' Kilpatrick shouted. 'He's still alive.' He cut the bonds and lowered him to the ground.'The stupid sonuvabitch. What did I tell him?'

'Yeah, I guess you were right,' Charlie muttered, as Tom splashed water from his canteen on his face and put it to his lips. 'Jeez,' he groaned. 'What a way to earn an honest buck.'

There was another rhythmic drumming of hooves, and the two Pinkerton men pulled their guns, expecting trouble. But, it was a young woman riding side-saddle on a spirited pony, galloping along the trail, reining in, expertly, in a swirl of dust when she saw them. 'Is he . . . all right?' she asked, breathlessly.

'Why?' Tom Patterson asked. 'Who are you?'

'Just a friend, I guess,' she breathed, slipping from her horse to kneel beside Charlie. 'We met this afternoon.'

'You did?' Kilpatrick screeched. 'Jeez. He's a fast worker.'

Hetty had paused long enough to grab a small medical aid tin she kept in the cottage. She hadn't even bothered putting on a hat or coat. Just saddled her pony and headed after him. Now she opened the tin and, borrowing the canteen of water, began dabbing cotton wool at Durango's cut and bruised face. 'Poor man,' she murmured.

Charlie opened his eyes and looked into Hetty's. 'So, it's true,' he said. 'There is a heaven. An angel of mercy before my eyes.' Only his words didn't come out very clear because his lips were starting to puff up from the beating.

'You've lost a tooth, man,' Tom said, as Durango spat blood. 'One of your canines.'

'Saves cost of the dentist,' Charlie mumbled. 'That one's been botherin' me long time. I'll be OK, rest up coupla days. Feels like coupla ribs stove in.'

Hetty was gently washing his facial wounds when she saw his hands. 'Goodness! Those burns! What have they done to you? *How could they*?'

'Easy,' Charlie said. 'There was twenty of them and one of me.'

'Look at his nails. It's disgusting. They're brutes.'

'Yeah, that weren't very nice. Chinese torture — aagh!' Charlie howled. 'No! Leave 'em be. They'll be OK.'

'Hold still,' she whispered. 'I'll just put some ointment on and bandage them. Why did they do this? Who are you?'

'Former US marshal turned Pinkerton agent. Guess there ain't no harm in telling you now. I mighta fooled you, honey, but I sure didn't fool them Renos.'

Hetty blushed at the way he drawled 'honey', the word curling warm inside her, making her feel good. She met his grey eyes and knew that there was a man who wouldn't just want her for his own ends. Here was a man who would treat a woman good all the time, not just when it suited him. Why, she wondered, had fate decreed she had to be a bad man's woman? She flickered a smile at him, and a tear fell from her eyes. 'I got some plaster in my tin. I can bind up your ribs.'

'Sure, honey, I'm in your hands.'

'My name's Hetty.'

'You say you and Frank Reno engaged?'

'Yes,' she nodded, lowering her eyes, ashamed, to her task. 'Well, more than that. I'm his woman. We're lovers.'

Durango was silent for a bit, only giving a gasp as she tugged the tape across his leanly muscled flesh. 'You going back to him?'

'I guess. That's the way it is.'

'You've made a bad bet,' Kilpatrick said. 'He ain't got no future. We're going to raise a posse in New Albany. We'll be back to take him, and his brothers.'

'Look,' Durango drawled, as he eased his back up against a boulder. 'Maybe that won't work. They got a hell of a lot of gunmen guarding that town. Maybe, Hetty, you should tell Frank and John that they can do a deal. Nobody's been killed yet. They ain't gonna be hanged. If the Renos give themselves up we might be able to arrange they only draw a short term in jail.'

'Really?' Hetty buttoned Durango's shirt for him. 'You want me to pass that message on?'

'Yeah, tell John and Frank they can't go on the way they are. It's only going to lead to bloodshed.'

'Aw that's no good,' Kilpatrick said.

'Will I see you again?' Hetty asked, as she went to get on her pony. 'It's getting dusk. I better be getting back.'

'Sure.' Durango forced a grin. 'I left my best Capper and Capper in that town. A twenty-dollar hat. And my Paterson. I'm mighty fond of that gun.'

6

Frank Reno, in his dandified gambler's clothes, the black coat cut away for easy access to the Smith and Wesson on his belt, was waiting for Hetty when she came trotting back on her pony, Candy. He cut a sinister figure in the dusk, his pale face gaunt, his black hair and jutting beard, his dark staring eyes. 'Where you been?' he whispered, huskily.

'I been to give aid to that poor man you beat so severely,' she said, slipping down and leading her pony into the stable.

'You *what*?' he shouted, grabbing hold of her arm. 'Don't walk away from me. What have you been up to?'

Hetty put the pony in his stall and turned to face him, defiantly. 'How could you do that to his hands, his nails? What have you become, some brute?'

Frank chopped her a back-hander across the cheek. 'Keep your nose out of our affairs.'

Hetty put her hand up to her smarting cheek. 'This is my town as well as yours. People don't like what's going on here. These *are* our affairs.'

She pushed past him and went into her cottage, lit the kerosene lamp, as he followed her. 'I'd rather you didn't come in. I'd like to be alone.'

'I'm sorry.' Frank grabbed hold of her, pulled her into him, starting into her face, falsely persuasive as he stroked her cheek. 'But you shouldn't go interfering. You've angered me. That man deserved all he got.'

'That man is a Pinkerton agent. And there were two more with him. Oh, Frank, what's got into you? Can't you see you can't go on like this? Men like those, they won't give up. They'll hunt you down.'

'Pinkerton man, eh? We had an idea

he was something like that. Well, now he knows what to expect.'

'Frank, they told me to tell you. It's not too late. They know you're not killers. If you and John give yourselves up they will help you. They will get you off with a light sentence. Why don't you talk to them?'

'Talk to them?'

'Yes, I believe they're men of their word. They said you might only have to serve a short term, maybe five years. I would wait for you. We could go away someplace else. We could still do what we planned to do.'

'Yeah?' He gave a doubtful sigh. 'You think so? You think they'd keep their word? Maybe I'll talk to Big John. He ain't happy with the way things are, no more than I am, no more than you are. Come on now, you light the fire, make me some supper, we'll — '

'No.' She pulled away from him. 'Not tonight. I'm tired.'

'Hey.' He pulled a diamond choker from his pocket. 'Look what I bought you. This cost me a small fortune.'

'Bought with somebody else's cash.' Hetty pouted her lips, shook her head, 'I don't want it. I don't want to look like your fancy woman. Frank, don't you see, I'm ashamed? I can't hold my head high in this town. It's not just the dishonesty, it's the . . . well, you seduced me into doing things I didn't ought to do, you promised me . . . '

'Aw, that. The usual woman's whines. I've told you we'll get wed once I get settled. Come on, Hetty, get the fire lit. I'll go split some logs. We'll stay in tonight, all nice and cosy, cuddled up.'

She put her fingers to her still smarting cheek. 'You ever hit me again, then, I warn you, I'll never let you touch me.'

'I've said I'm sorry. You want me to crawl? You got me riled. Come on, gal, cook me up something nice. I love that li'l stewpot of your'n.'

Hetty blushed. 'The things you say. I know you only want me for that.' She tried to push him away as he squeezed her waist, kissed her cheek. 'Oh, very well. I guess I got to forgive you. This won't get supper fixed. Go on, there's the axe. Go take out your energy on the logs.'

When he had gone outside she touched her cheek again and shook her head. 'Strong man like that shouldn't hit a gal,' she said. 'It ain't right. And I didn't like what they did to that feller.' Maybe she should face it: Frank Reno frightened her.

★ ★ ★

The three Pinkerton agents headed back south, riding for fifty miles over two days, taking it easy, for Charlie Durango, with his swollen face, and bandaged fingers and ribs, was not in the best of shape. However, he managed to stay in the saddle. Well, he had been practically born in it, it was his second home. He even mumbled a song as he thought of Hetty, something

about, 'The sweet rose of Indiana . . . '
But, maybe, it occurred to him, she
wasn't as sweet as she looked. Never a
rose without plenty of thorns. And she
was the paramour of a vicious robber.
Maybe it was best to forget Hetty.

They ambled their horses into the
larger town of New Albany, a more
important halt than Seymour on the
main railroad connection to the south.
The town had just built a two-storey
sheriff's office and jailhouse there of
real bricks, instead of flimsy wood like
most of the buildings.

'Nobody ain't gonna bust out of
here,' the sheriff, Tom Stone, a big-
jawed, ruddy-faced man boasted. 'And
we don't allow no layabouts to take over
our town like they done up in Seymour.
That so-called sheriff of their'n, Abe
Wappenshaw, I allus known he was a
bag of horse manure.' He cleared his
throat and spat loudly and excessively,
to emphasize his point.

'Mr Stone, would you be ready to
raise a posse and help us clear out that

nest of rats?' Tom Patterson asked.

'Sir, I'd be happy to. Ain't had no action in a long time.'

★ ★ ★

Hetty Hancock was sprawled half-asleep at dawn, some three days later, when she was brought fully awake by the shuddering of the ground by horses' hooves as they galloped by, a yelling and blood-thirsty ya-hooing, and loud gunshot blasts.

Frank Reno raised himself by one arm, peering over her out of the window. 'Ye gods,' he muttered. 'What's going on?'

Hetty raised the curtain and peered out at the last of the riders dashing by, six-guns gripped in their fists. 'Oh my God!' she cried. 'What have you brought upon us now?'

'Who in tarnation are they?' Frank asked, grabbing to pull on his shirt and clothes. 'What right they got to come busting in here?'

'They got the right of law,' she replied, brushing her hair from her face, looking distraught. 'They're after you and your brothers, Frank.'

'Too bad,' he grinned. 'Jest as well they didn't know I was in here with my l'il turtle-dove or they'd have caught me with my pants down.' He tugged on his boots, reached for the Winchester carbine, levered it to snap a round in, and headed for the door. He peered out along the street. 'There must be nearly forty of 'em.' He put a strong hand to the nape of her head, jerked her face to him and kissed her, wildly, before she could protest. 'You stay hid. Wish me luck, gal.'

Hetty watched him go running away, dodging behind hedges and trees, kneeling to fire the Winchester at the backs of the mounted men, making them wheel their mounts with surprise and return fire. And saw him go dashing across the main street, firing as he ran, heading for the saloon, hurling himself, bodily, through its window before they could cut him down.

Hetty bit her lip. 'The fool,' she whispered. 'He's crazy. He'll never get away.'

★ ★ ★

Frank Reno arrived in the saloon in a crash of glass to find Abel Finnegan and Miles Ogle already firing their long-arm Kentucky pieces out of the bat-wing doorway. They had spent their night dozing on the saloon sofa. 'Yee-hoo!' Abel shrieked. 'Durn near got one. Why don't they hold still?'

Jesse Thompson and Frank's cousin, Trick Reno, were dashing in from the back of the saloon, ducking low as bullets poured in from outside, smashing mirrors and bottles. 'Get over at the window,' Frank shouted, pausing to pick up a beheaded bottle of bourbon and dash upstairs. He put the broken neck to his mouth, and gasped as the fiery brew hit him. 'Right, let me at 'em,' he yelled.

Big John was already at the window of his bedroom aiming his Winchester at the horsemen galloping backwards and forwards below. Frank kneeled beside him and took aim at a lanky rider he vaguely recognized. His slug ploughed into his shoulder, knocking him from his mount, and he lay, his hat fallen away, his raw spotty face staring up at him. Frank levered the Winchester to finish him, but the man on the ground met his eyes, and raised a Spencer carbine to snap off a shot at him. Frank was forced to duck back as the bullet splintered the woodwork by his head.

When he peered out again he saw a stockier rider in a bearskin coat charging his horse back, and putting out an arm to haul the lanky one up behind him. They went bouncing away down the street, and Frank aimed the Winchester at their backs, but missed.

'Glory alley-loo-ya!' Big John roared, as his Winchester slug tore into the chest of a horse ridden by a man he knew to be the sheriff of New Albany, Tom Stone. The mustang screamed and showed its teeth in a snarl of pain as blood poured from its chest and it rolled over, hooves flailing. Stone nimbly stepped from the saddle and ran like a jack-rabbit for cover behind a horse trough. Big John smashed bullets into it, laughing hysterically. 'Serve you right, you sinner. Damnation on you. Get back to where you belong.'

He raised his fist to heaven. 'Praise be the Lord. How the mighty are fallen.'

Frank glanced at him, as he found boxes of ammunition in a dresser drawer. Sometimes he wondered if Big John was quite right in the head. He tossed a box across, and began to expertly fill his own magazine. 'Kill the horses. Shoot them from under them,' John shouted. 'Don't break the commandments or we'll all go to hell.'

Over in the railroad depot the rugged old Civil War sergeant, Charlie

Spencer, aided by Albert Perkins and Billy Biggers, were giving little credence to this advice. They were shooting to kill, and they provided a withering crossfire. That, allied to the rifle fire from guards posted on rooftops, a constant hail of gunfire, in fact, were giving the men on horseback second thoughts. They backed away to safety, firing revolvers or carbines as they went.

The posse was composed of ranchers, farmers, shopkeepers, ordinary men, who had set out determined to smoke the Renos out. They had had the optimism of men setting out on a 'coon hunt. Now, as lead whistled dangerously close about their heads, as they saw blood spurt from the arms and legs of their compatriots, they wheeled their horses in confusion. Several of the poor beasts had tumbled dead into the dirt. They realized this was not going to be an easy picnic.

The outlaws were not without their casualties. Trick Reno howled, piteously, as lead cut across his knuckles. His cousin Wilk fell back with a hole in his side, staring with incomprehension at the blood on his hand. 'I been hit,' he croaked.

Simeon and William were not having it easy, either, for the position they had taken behind an overturned wagon was under attack from the rear, from the windows of Jones' emporium. Simeon turned and caught sight of Major Ike McLaury with a six-gun blazing in his fist. He flattened himself back against the wagon as bullets cut across his chest and William crawled for the safety of a water butt. Hyram Jones and Doc Dooley had also joined in the fray, but their aim was poor, and their shots were putting the fear of God into the posse-riders instead of the Renos.

'Back off, men,' the big-jawed New Albany sheriff, Tom Stone, shouted. 'The bastards kilt my hoss. How'm I goin' to git home?'

'You'll have to ride two-up, like us,' Tom Patterson answered, as he and Kilpatrick scrambled from their remaining mount and sought cover in Hetty Hancock's garden. 'Kilpatrick's in a bad way. I hate to say it, but I think they got us beat. We're going to have to call this a day.'

'A day? Some bloody day! At least none of us are dead yet. It's a miracle we ain't,' Stone said. 'Why didn't you warn me they had all these damn blasted guns? Oh, excuse me, ma'am.'

Hetty had come out from the house with a bowl of hot water and her ambulance box under her arm. She had got used to treating casualties after the war as they wended their way home along the trail to the north. 'If you'll cease your shouting and get out of the way I might be able to do something for this man.' She knelt down beside Kilpatrick and examined his wound. 'I think he's going to be lucky, thanks to merciful God. The bullet's gone clean through. All I can do is bandage him up and you'd better get him back to a hospital before gangrene sets in.'

The rest of the posse had dodged away on foot, finding cover along the street, and the shooting had become a desultory stalemate. Most men were fast running out of ammunition.

Hetty turned her dark eyes on Patterson. 'I thought you said you were going to offer us a deal. This is no way to do it.'

'It was worth a try,' Tom grunted. 'But I guess they got us beat. Come on, men, we'll commandeer a wagon and hosses for the wounded and head back.'

'Sure thang,' Tom Stone growled, his enthusiasm dampened. 'That was a fifty-dollar hoss of mine they shot. This ain't nuthin' to do with us, anyhow. It ain't my territ'ry.'

He trudged away, calling to his men to put up their guns. He tied a white handkerchief around his carbine and waved it towards the saloon. 'We're pulling out,' he shouted. 'You gonna let us take our wounded?'

'Take 'em and go, you godless

scum,' Big John roared from his window. 'And don't try tangling with us again. We run this town. You'd better believe that.'

'You win,' Stone shouted back. 'For today.' He hauled up one of his gunfighters, with a bullet through his thigh, and helped him hobble away, while other of the walking wounded crawled from their hidey-holes and limped after him.

'Look at the curs, crawling away like whipped dogs,' Big John laughed, 'their tails between their legs.'

Sheriff Abe Wappenshaw had been cowering in his office all this time, and now he unlocked and stepped out. 'How's it going?' he asked, looking at the shattered glass, sniffing at the rolling clouds of powder smoke. 'You boys been havin' fun?'

The Renos had stepped out into the road and strode across to Hyram Jones' emporium. 'Come on out,' Frank called.

Major Ike McLaury, in frock-coat

and former campaign hat, stepped out, holstering his six-gun. He stood to attention before the Renos, while Doc Dooley and Hyram Jones joined him more sheepishly. 'Bad luck, boys,' Frank said. 'You backed the wrong side. Your pals have gone.' He jabbed his carbine into the major's abdomen and, as he doubled up, kneed him in the face, knocking him to the ground. He caught hold of Jones by his thinning hair and hurled him back towards his ruined shop. 'Clear off,' he snarled. 'Think yourselves lucky we don't shoot you.'

At that point Clinton Reno came riding into town. 'Hello,' he grinned. 'I heard the shootin' miles away. What's been going on?'

'Look at him,' Simeon said. 'We been doing all the work, risking our lives, while he's been getting his end away.'

'Well, nobody told me I was wanted. You should have sent a smoke signal. That widow lady she's mighty friendly, specially when I showed her my persuader.'

Young Clinton was finding that being in a position of power, with a revolver on his hip, and being ruggedly good-looking, in a bearish way, he could have his way with quite a few of the ladies in the vicinity. He didn't consider it sinful because he only forced them to service him in a non-penetrative way, so he wasn't harming anybody. 'Boys,' Clinton said, with his cheerful grin, 'I been thinking of standing for senator, maybe even president. That way I could have any gal I wanted, any day of the week.'

'Grow up,' Big John growled, for, although they had won the day, he was feeling considerably rattled by the attack. 'Ain't you any idea what that kind of behaviour can do to you? All medical wisdom is agreed that over-indulgence, the loss of essential fluids, sends a man blind and demented. Just go take a look in a madhouse, you'll see proof of that.'

Clinton smirked at his younger brothers behind Big John's back and touched his temple. John was too much like their puritanical father for his taste. Simeon and William, too, were more easy-going, had duded themselves up in striped pants, natty boots, red wool shirts and leather jackets, intent on having a good time with the 'poor trash' girls, who had been drawn as by a magnet to Seymour and its free-spending outlaws.

Some of these 'nymphs' looked mighty shaken by the attack on the town as they bustled around the saloon amid the shambles of broken glass and splintered woodwork, trying to help Hetty attend to the men who had received flesh-wounds.

'Who's going to pay for all this damage?' Harry Holt, the owner of the Red Garter, demanded, as he looked in dismay at his smashed bottles, and the beer trickling from the bullet holes in a barrel. He had provided the girls with rooms in the attic and was taking a cut in their profits.

'Fear not. Here.' Big John opened his cashbox and tossed him a wad of a hundred dollars. 'Buy some more booze. We have had a great victory. It is a day to celebrate. We smote the Philistines a mighty blow. Line up, boys, it's pay-day. Y'all get a twenty-dollar bonus. You done well.'

As his men scrambled to get their share, Big John told them, 'Nobody got killed, so nobody is going to get hanged. Remember, that's the way we Renos do it. Y'all can shoot the eye out of a squirrel, so shoot to hit the thigh, the arm, the shoulder, if necessary, but not to kill. That way some of us might have to do a short term up the river, but that will pass. What's important is nobody will have an excuse to put rope around our necks.'

Hetty glanced at the girls and raised her eyes to heaven. 'Do you really believe that?' she said to Frank.

Outside, the citizens of Seymour were standing in shocked groups discussing

101

the gunfight. Hyram Jones was using his broom, trying to clear up the mess made of his store. His wife was clucking like a nervous hen telling him they ought to pack up and go. Sam Ingram, the butcher, was hauling away with a team the dead horses round to the back of his yard. Their steaks would soon be hanging from the hooks in his store. The children had been warned to keep away from the saloon and rail depot, but were running about, excitedly, playing gunfights, the teenage boys keen to emulate the Renos' notoriety.

Hetty finished bandaging the worst hit, Will Reno, and walked across to her own store to inspect the damage. The women in their sunhats and long dresses turned away, disapproving, as she passed. The window had been smashed by flying bullets, but most of her stock was unharmed. So she put up a notice on a dummy in the window, 'Business as usual.' Trade had perked up, for, if the local ladies were cutting her, the young hussies who arrived to hustle in the saloon were keeping her busy supplying blouses, dresses and petticoats. They had descended on her like a flock of loose-tongued birds demanding the latest in fashionable hats, scarlet stockings and skimpy drawers. Hetty disapproved of the foolish, flighty things, but, business was business, she guessed. Whatever, her sewing needle had never been so busy.

In spite of the cheesy looks cast her way, Hetty attended Sunday service as was her wont. The parson, a wan-faced man with a wart on his nose, looked somewhat alarmed when Big John stomped into church and propped his Winchester against the pew in the front row. Frank joined her, smart, as always, in black suit and clean linen. Big John sang lustily, shaking the church rafters. The parson took his sermon from the New Testament on how the meek would inherit the earth. John preferred the brimstone and fire of the Old Testament and suddenly roared, 'Blessed be the Lord my strength, which teacheth my hand to war and my finger to fight.' In the stunned silence he got up and walked out.

In the parlance of later times John Reno would probably have been diagnosed as a manic-depressive or schizophrenic. He had, at first, been elated by the way they had sent the posse running. He had even grabbed one of the 'nymphs' and done a jig around the saloon. But then he had got mad and banished them all to the barn. He sat bowed over a bowl of hot water for 'the vapours', rubbing onion juice into his balding scalp, sunk into a trough of depression. He had been to see an old woman in a cabin in the woods, who claimed to be able to raise the dead, as in Samuel, and see the future. She had prophesied that he would travel over water to a strange island, that his family would be lost to him. It filled him with gloom. The old woman extracted twenty dollars from

John, told him to beware stepping on people's shadows, and to recommend his brothers to see her.

'I been talking to the Lord,' John announced. 'He tells me it's time I parleyed with the enemy. Otherwise they ain't gonna give us no peace at all. I got to take the sins of my family on my own shoulders to protect you all.'

'If that's the way you want it, John,' Frank said.

'That's the way I want it. We'll go over to the depot and send a telegraph to Pinkerton in Chicago. If he comes down here alone I'll talk to him.'

'Good,' Hetty said, when Frank told her. 'You know it makes sense.'

7

A telegraph arrived back from Chicago the following day:

JOHN RENO STOP WILL ARRIVE SEYMOUR RAIL DEPOT TOMORROW ELEVEN AM STOP HAVE GOVERNORS AUTHORITY TO OFFER AMNESTY IF YOU AGREE TO SURRENDER STOP FOR REASONS OF SAFETY TALKS TO BE HELD ON BOARD FLYER STOP I WILL BE ALONE AS YOU MUST BE STOP ALLAN PINKERTON

The brothers pored over it and Frank told Big John, 'It sounds like they just want you to give yourself up and the rest of us go free.'

'It's probably a trick,' William opined.

'I don't know.' Big John stared at the telegraph as if trying to divine its true meaning. 'It seems fair enough. I guess he wants to stay on the train 'cause he's scared we might take a pot at him if he steps outa line. I guess we gotta trust 'em.'

'Maybe,' Clinton said, 'they just want us to stop robbin' their trains. Maybe if we agreed not to harass them they'd give us a big pay-off?'

'You'd be lucky,' Simeon put in. 'But if the big shot's coming all the way down here to see us, we'd better hear him out.'

'Look, boys, if it's just a case of me doing a short stretch, like those detectives said, then that's OK by me,' Big John told them. 'If the Governor's given his word that's fair enough. After all, we're only going to talk about it, ain't we?'

They were waiting over at the saloon the next morning, the five Renos, and their gang, as The Flyer pulled in dead on time. The great locomotive, its bell clanging mournfully, slid to a halt, and stood there, its engine susurrating. There was only one Pullman carriage, which appeared to be empty, apart from one man, in a grey suit and derby, who was at the open door. There wasn't even a conductor, only a fireman and engineer, who leaned from the cab, watching.

The sharp-faced Allan Pinkerton saluted and shouted out, 'Here I am, John Reno. If you want to talk, come on over. By yourself, not with your men.'

Big John stood up, the twin Remingtons cross-slung, a double belt of bullets around his waist. He scratched at his beard and growled, 'Here I go, boys. I wonder what the l'il gopher's gonna offer us. You hang on here.'

Allan Pinkerton smiled as he approached and called, 'there'll be just the two of us. I'm sure we can hammer something out.' He offered his hand and shook John Reno's, warmly. 'Good to meet you. Let's go inside.'

He led him into a luxurious stateroom, with polished walnut cladding, sofas and chairs, and a bar at one end. 'What's it to be, Mr Reno? Whiskey? Take a chair.'

As Big John did so he felt a jolting movement, and, looking out of the window, saw that the train was in motion. 'What's going on?' He went for his right-hand gun, but Pinkerton had turned from the bar with a derringer in his hand. There was a puff of smoke and a small-calibre bullet cut into John's wrist, making him drop his gun.

Simultaneously, a sofa-bed that folded into the wall swung down and Charlie Durango rolled out, a short-barrelled Colt Navy in his hand and pointed at Big John.

John Reno had gone for his left-hand gun and it was half-out of its holster when Durango whispered, 'I wouldn't do that if I were you. Not if you want to live.'

At the same time the doors at front and rear of the carriage opened and Tom Patterson and another Pinkerton agent appeared, Spencer carbines in their hands, the business ends levelled at him.

The locomotive engine was blasting out steam at a thumping rate and the train was getting up speed. Big John stood up, his hands outstretched, as if to surrender, and lunged for Charlie's gun, which exploded as they wrestled for possession.

The bullet whistled past Patterson's ear, and he didn't dare fire because Big John had swung the lanky Westerner around to use as a shield. The only thing to do was to pile in and try to hold him, which they all did. Big John roared like a bull, and bucked like one, too, kicking out and getting Pinkerton in the groin, making him grovel away. He swung the three other men back and forth as the train swayed with them, and they all went tumbling and crashing into the bar. Tom had his arm around Reno's throat and his fingers gouging at his eyes. The other agent was hauling on one of his kicking legs. Charlie hung onto the revolver which exploded again, putting an airhole in the ceiling.

But the strength of Big John was no match for three determined men, who dragged him down, sitting on him, trying to avoid his snapping teeth and flailing fists. Finally they got him disarmed and manacled hand and foot, and he lay there breathing hard. 'You sons of bitches,' he said. 'You gave me your word.'

Meanwhile, the Reno brothers on the steps of the Red Garter had watched open-jawed as The Flyer had pulled away. They ran over to try to jump on it, but were too late. It was bobbing away along the rail, heading north, its stack shooting up a column of grey smoke.

'They got Big John,' Charlie Spencer shouted, as if that were not painfully obvious, and he, and a couple of the boys, went to leap on their mustangs and give chase. Normally, they might have caught up, whipping their horses flat out up to speeds of thirty miles an hour, but, with only one lightweight carriage to pull, and on the plain, The

Flyer had capitalized on its surprise start and was reaching high speed, leaving the horsemen in its wake.

Frank suddenly heard the steam whistle of another locomotive coming from the south. He turned and saw a local stopping train easing in from New Albany. 'Uncouple those cars,' he shouted at a conductor who jumped off.

'What for? What these passengers gonna do?'

Frank put his Smith and Wesson to his head. 'Just do as I say. Savvy?' He ran to climb up beside the driver and, with the revolver stuck up his nose, shouted, 'Get ready to go. And go fast. We got no time to lose. We gotta catch up with The Flyer in front.'

'Why so?' the fireman asked. 'What's the hurry?'

'Don't ask questions. Just start tossing in wood. I want full steam ahead. There's five hundred dollars for you if we catch 'em. Come on, boys, get up on the tender,' he shouted at

112

several of his men. 'They ain't gonna get away with this.'

The outlaws gave wild whoops as they hung onto the rocking tender, tossing logs down to the fireman. 'There she is,' Frank shouted. 'She ain't so far ahead.' The Flyer had been slowed by the curving incline out of Seymour — where they had once blocked the track — and they were gaining on her. Perhaps they weren't yet aware they were being pursued? Or, maybe, without any carriages at all to pull, their engine had the advantage.

The men began wildly shooting their carbines and rifles to little purpose, but out of sheer excitement as they drew near to the rear of The Flyer. The wheels were racketing away on the rails, the rods pumping, the engine straining and gasping, coughing out smoke as the driver took the incline full throttle. They were almost up to the back of it. 'Go on, ram it,' Frank shouted above the uproar.

But The Flyer had reached the incline

and was heading down the other side. A white-haired and moustached lawman had stepped out on the observation platform and was aiming his Henry. His bullets 'pa-danged' and ricocheted about their heads. The bell was clanging madly as the outlaws sent a fusillade back. They groaned with disappointment as The Flyer began to draw away.

'What's the matter?' Frank demanded.

'They got more power than us. They're opening up.'

Helplessly, Frank Reno watched as The Flyer increased the distance between them, half a mile, one mile, almost two miles away in the distance going straight as an arrow across the countryside, bearing his brother inexorably away. But on they chugged, chasing after it.

Suddenly they sighted The Flyer ahead. It had stopped beside a wooden tank tower to take on water. 'Now we've got them,' Frank shouted in jubilation. Their own engine thundered up the line, its whistle screaming, and the outlaws cocked their guns in readiness. The fireman of The Flyer swung the rubber nozzle aside, and left it with water gushing out, as his engine moved them away again, thrusting its smoke into the blue sky.

'Hot damn,' Frank shouted. 'Keep on going, after them!'

'We need water, too,' the engineer shouted. 'And if we don't hurry we won't be getting none.'

The water was pouring out in a flood from the abandoned rubber hose adjoining the tank and Charlie Durango had not helped by hanging from the back of The Flyer and pounding his heavy calibre Henry bullets to smash holes in the wood, stoving it in so it leaked like a cullender.

By the time the fireman had got the hose linked up with their own engine it was too late. The tower was dry.

'Can't you go on to the next one?' Frank asked.

'Why you think they call this a steam engine? No water, no steam.'

The driver shrugged and wiped his face with a rag. 'Looks to me like you boys have got a long walk home.'

★ ★ ★

'There's a telegraph message for you, Mistuh Reno,' Hank Diprose said as Frank and his boys limped back into Seymour.

EVER BEEN HAD STOP YOU ARE NEXT ON OUR LIST STOP PINKERTON

Frank's face contorted, puce with anger. He crumbled the message up and went over to the saloon, calling for a bottle of bourbon. He soaked his blistered feet in a bowl of hot water, smoked a cigar and stared at the bottle. 'John was right,' he growled, his face like thunder. 'The perfidy of man is beyond belief.'

He cabled money to pay for the smartest lawyer and waited as John Reno was arraigned before the courts with due process. He cabled the governor, demanding to know if he and his brothers had been granted an amnesty. He fumed as he received no reply.

One morning Clinton came running over waving copies of the *Chicago Tribune* that had just been dropped off the train. 'John Reno Gets Forty Years Hard Labour' the banner headline screamed.

'Big John goes down, but why are his train-robbing, bank-robbing brothers allowed to go free?' ran an editorial on the front page. 'No other state would tolerate this situation. For too long the Renos have terrorized Southern Indiana. Now is the time for action.'

'It's not fair.' Clinton had tears streaming down his cheeks. 'They promised us a deal. Frank, what are we gonna do?'

'Do?' Frank's dark eyes glinted, maniacally. 'They think they cut off the head they can kill the rooster?

How wrong can they be? I'm gonna be the new head. And I'm gonna have my revenge.' He picked up a horsewhip. 'Think they can laugh, do they? I'm gonna teach this town a lesson.'

He strode out of the saloon over to Hyram Jones' emporium, running him by the scruff of his neck out into the street. 'Think you're mayor of this town, do you?' He cracked the whip and began thrashing him, mercilessly, as his wife begged and screamed. 'You're nobody. None of you.'

His whiskeyed-up men rode back and forth rowdying up the town, shooting revolvers, smashing windows and street lights. Folks scurried indoors, banging closed their shutters. Abe Wappenshaw hurried back into his jailhouse. Frank swung onto his Morgan and raced at the head of his brothers out of town. They galloped into Major McLaury's property and set fire to his barns. Frank, his face set in a bitter smile, watched as McLaury tried to save his horses and cattle, as his winter hay went up, as his chickens scurried out from the flames and foolishly ran back in again.

Major McLaury, and his grey-haired spinster sister, stood and watched as the Renos rode away. 'Something's got to be done about them,' he said, hoarsely.

Hetty was ashen-faced as Frank climbed from his Morgan by her cottage gate. 'You — you dare to come here?'

'You,' he screamed, clutching her blouse at the throat and running her back into the house. 'You — you said he would only get five years.' He raised his hand as if to strike her, but threw her down on the bed.

'That's what I believed. How was I to know?'

'What? That your wonderful Pinkerton friends were all liars? Scum, that's all they are. My brother, at least, was a man of his word.'

'I'm sorry, Frank, sorry about John.

119

He didn't deserve that sentence. It is inhumane.'

'Sorry? Make peace with them, Frank,' he mimicked. 'You know its for the best. Well, there'll be no peace now.'

He was packing his shirts and cash into a saddle-bag. 'Where are you going?' she asked.

'We're leaving. They'll be after us now. But we'll be back and' — he pointed a finger at her — 'you can tell these people that if they give us any trouble we'll burn this town to the ground.' Before leaving, Frank called in at the depot. 'You got any information for us, Hank?'

'No, I'm sorry, sir. The railroad's changed its codes. I figure they gotten suspicious of me.'

'Don't worry.' Frank tossed him a wad of five hundred dollars 'Spread this around among the railroad clerks up the line. Don't go keeping it for yourself. Tell them it pays to help the Renos. Me and the boys are heading out west for a while. But we'll be back. You hear of any big shipments, you let me know.'

He rode out of Seymour at the head of a chosen few of his band of outlaws. 'We've got to forget about Big John. He's lost to us. He'll be seventy, an old man, when, or if, he ever gets out.'

'What was it that ole witch told him?' Will asked. 'That he'd be going over water? That bit's come true. They're shipping him to Riker's Island. Nobody's ever escaped from there.'

'At least he's still alive,' Clinton chimed in. 'They didn't hang him. He'll have plenty time to study his Bible.'

'Yes, he may be lost to us, but we're gonna carry on the way he'd want. No killing. That way we might save our necks, too.'

★ ★ ★

They ferried their fine horses across the Big River once more and headed up through Iowa, drifting through winter snows to Ottumwa, Oscaloosa, along the Skunk River to Marshalltown and Fort Dodge. If anyone questioned them they claimed to be cowhands and horse dealers heading for Nebraska. Frank and his brothers still had some dollars left from the Missouri hold-up. He frittered what was left of his on general expenses and gambling, keeping an ear open all the time for the possibility of a big hit.

They rode on through Indian country to Pocohontas, Cherokee and Sioux Rapids, and across to Sioux City on the Missouri River. They had no idea that a white-haired former marshal and two Pinkerton agents were picking up their trail, persistently tracking them. It was in Sioux City that an army deserter called Jimmy Dunlap told Frank about a place called Magnolia and a bank that was waiting to be busted. All he needed was their help.

'We're not interested in anything small-time,' Frank said. 'What's the take likely to be? And how do you know this?'

Dunlap raised his eyebrows with a knowing look. 'Pretty gal works in the bank told me. She and me, well, we were going to run away together. This was going to be like her dowry. Twenty thousand dollars. That's what's in that bank, just waiting to be taken.'

The Renos looked at each other, at their trusted lieutenants, Charlie Spencer, Miles Ogle, and Mike Rogers, and at the seven assorted riff-raff who made up their band. 'Let's ride,' Frank said.

The Renos were proud of the fact that they had never killed. Mainly it was because they had never had their hand forced. They didn't need to. When they entered a saloon, the brothers and their cohorts, armed to the teeth, looked around, eyes narrowed, checking all those there, it would be a brave man who would not step back and make room for them at the bar. And a braver one still who would challenge them to a gunfight. Their menacing presence made any room they entered fall silent. They could handle guns and they had a past. And it showed. Once an obstreperous drunk had pulled a six-gun on Frank. He had wrested it from his grasp and buffaloed him with it, stepping over his unconscious body without a word.

The fanciful idea of two men facing up to each other out on the street for a gun duel was not prevalent in the West. Most killings occurred when a man in a drunken rage got in first before the other had a chance. Numerous US Marshals had been gunned down, and a hundred more would be before the century was out, but most were bushwhacked, or shot in the back. Frank could take a man's earlobe off at thirty paces with a revolver, but he hadn't needed to yet.

So they employed their customary menacing tactics when they approached the Harrison County Bank in Magnolia the next morning, riding slow into town, leaving two of the boys holding the horses, and bursting in, carbines at the ready, covering all inside. They were the first customers.

A pretty blonde girl, demurely dressed, looked up from her ledger book, into the pistol barrel of Jimmy Dunlap. 'Hi, Katie,' he grinned. 'Missed me?'

'You? What are you doing here?' When she realized he was acting on the information she had supplied, she hissed, 'You — you lousy double-crossing piece of — '

'Language, Katie, language! Now you just ask these people to stay nice and quiet and keep their hands where we can see them. And start filling these sacks of our'n with all the cash you got in here.'

The manager, fat and full of himself, protested, until Frank put the barrel of his Smith and Wesson in his mouth and stroked his bald head. 'Just give us the keys to the vault, sweetheart. Or are you looking to have your brains spattered over the wall?'

The younger clerks gave no trouble. As well as bills there were a couple of sacks of silver coin to haul out. The heist went like a dream, like clockwork. The staff were told to lay face down on the floor and stay there, and Frank led his boys out.

And then someone shouted, 'They're robbing the bank!', and men ran from the barbershop and the billiard hall and started shooting at them. Their horses whinnied and skittered, and they were hard put to haul themselves into their saddles. But they set off at a gallop, firing revolvers and carbines at the men on the side-walk, racing out of town. And again nobody had got hurt. 'Yee-haugh!' Clinton yelled, expressing the excitement and elation they all felt as they spurred their horses into a fast lope. 'Let's git outa here.'

8

They were in high spirits until Simeon Reno happened to turn in his saddle and glance back. 'Hey! There's a posse behind us.'

The others hauled their mounts in. It was a wild country of grey, granite cliffs, and they had climbed a rise to cross a spur cutting across their path. The thaw had set in but there were still fields of snow in the shadow. And two miles back they could see the snow being churned up by a considerable body of men on horseback, hard on their tail.

Abel, in his coonskin cap and over-large over-coat, thonged by a leather gunbelt, called, in his high-pitched voice, 'Durn me, if it's a chase they lookin' fer, we kin give 'em it.'

It was the signal to set off, whipping their horses into a faster lope. It was noon, the sun a faint lemon in a grey misty sky. They had been riding for two hours and their mounts were about ready for a breather. They couldn't afford to push them too hard. The Morgans were all heart and would go for another thirty or so miles, but only the Renos and Spencer were mounted on them, the others on a varied collection of mustangs. They crossed the spur and went charging down a sweeping stretch of rocky grassland, heading across a high plain.

An hour later they slowed their mounts and turned to look again. In the far distance the band of pursuers were still there, packed tight together and determined. 'They ain't gonna give up,' William Reno said, showing the white in his eyes. 'What we gonna do, Frank?'

Frank tugged at his jutting goatee. 'Maybe we can give 'em the slip. You know this country, Dunlap. Where 'n hell are we?'

'We're headin' for Council Bluffs.'

Dunlap, still wearing his ex-soldier's greatcoat and a forage cap, pointed up a narrow canyon. 'Look, maybe if we go up this coulée we can throw 'em off.'

'What if it don't lead nowhere?'

'Then we can make a stand,' Clinton grinned. 'We got plenty of ammo. We can blast 'em out of their saddles.'

'Hmm?' Frank glanced at his younger brothers. They had never been tried in battle. In fact, they had had it easy, up to now. 'There must be forty or fifty men. Cattlemen. They know this land. And they know how to shoot. Don't think they're going to be sitting ducks.'

'Aw, let's give it a try. We gotta do something.'

'Right.' Frank led them away up the canyon, walking his horse because the other mounts were sweated up and beginning to blow hard. He was not anxious for a confrontation with the men behind them. 'If this don't work out, don't blame me.'

Fortunately, the canyon led across the ridge, and there was a way down the other side, a narrow ledge of an Indian trail following a fault. They reached solid ground and set off again at a hard lope. The snow would not help them, revealing their tracks on the ground. But they were forced to cross frozen patches in the lee of the hills.

By mid-afternoon they had lost sight of any pursuers, turning from one canyon into another in this maze of hills, at one point going back over their own tracks. 'Where in tarnation we goin' to?' Abel asked. 'There ain't no way out.'

'Aw, quit whinin',' Frank said, adjusting the sack of silver across his mount's neck. It was in danger of spilling out. 'This is big country. We just keep going, we're certain to get someplace.'

'Yeah, maybe jail,' William said, not realizing how right he would be.

'Come on,' Frank shouted, and headed away, taking his direction from the fast-disappearing sun in its haze of mist. Their mounts were badly in need of rest and water, but he knew it was no use slowing their pace. 'We gotta get out of these damn hills.'

It was getting dark when the robbers ploughed down the rocky side of a hill, kicking up shale, and caught sight of a silver sliver of stream winding through a narrow valley. There was ice bordering its banks and they allowed their horses a brief drink of its icy water. 'What do you reckon this stream is?'

Dunlap stroked his stubbled jaw. 'Maybe the Little Sioux? We follow it downstream, we probably reach the Missouri.'

'Yeah,' Clinton scoffed. 'I reckon you know as much about that as I do.'

Frank led them along the stream, splashing through the water wherever possible to try to lose their tracks. He was getting worried about his stallion. He seemed to be troubled. He didn't have the usual spring in his step. He leaned down, patted his strong neck. 'Come on, boy.'

'Hey, Frank,' William called. 'Your stallion's cheatin' on his right leg. Looks like he might be wind-galled.'

Frank reined in, stepped down and took a look. 'Yeah,' he muttered. 'He don't look so good. We've crossed some hard country. I'm going to have to rest him up. Looks like you boys better go on without me.'

'We sure ain't doin' that,' Simeon yelled. 'You can ride behind me.'

'Two-up? No, that's no good. That'll slow you all down,' Frank said. 'This is mighty lonesome country. Maybe we oughta stash the cash someplace round here, under one of them big rocks. Come back for it when the coast is clear. There's a possibility we might run into that posse tomorrow. Those sort of boys ain't gonna give up. But if we don't have the loot they don't have a case. Or, looking at the blackest side, if we get sent

132

down we got something to come out to.'

'Nope. No way,' Dunlap snapped. 'I'm due to the biggest cut on this. I'm the one who set this up. You wouldn't have nuthin' if it weren't for me. You can do what you like with your share, but I ain't leavin' mine for one of these saddle trash to come and pick up. I want mine now and then I split. I go my own way.'

The younger Renos backed their horses away from him, and pulled back their coats ready to go for their guns. Dunlap scowled back, but stood his ground. 'What you say, Frank?' Clinton called.

Frank in his caped greatcoat and wide-brimmed hat was kneeling, soothing his stallion's flank. 'Maybe he's got a point. Maybe we should make the split and each go our own ways. That way we would confuse any pursuit. All my hoss needs is coupla days rest and I can make it on my own.'

'Ya! Ya! Ya!' Abel Finnegan was

shouting as he came charging back. He had ridden up ahead to spy the land. At first, they thought he had seen the posse, but no. 'There's a cabin up ahead. We can shivaree there tonight.'

It was almost dark so they followed him along, Frank walking his stallion. The log cabin was on a rise on the far side of the stream. It had a chimney of rock, but there was no smoke. 'Looks like it's empty.'

'It sure is,' Abel whooped. 'An' I'm mighty hungry.'

They unsaddled their tired horses and hobbled them to rough graze. They piled into the cabin, which had one bunk, and by the look of the rat droppings seemed to be deserted. They soon had a fire roaring in the grate, and sat around steaming out their clothes, chawing on hard-tack and jerky, washed down with hot black coffee.

'Boys,' Frank said. 'I think it's time to split the take.'

Their eyes gleamed greedily in the

firelight as he spilled the silver out onto the bunk and began to count. It was mostly in singles, fives, and ten-pieces. Next came the wads of notes, one hundred dollars in each. It took some figuring but they finally worked it out at fourteen thousand dollars.

'Whee-eee!' William whistled. 'We're in the money again.'

'Yeah.' Clinton rolled a five dollar note, held it to the fire to catch, and lit his cheroot. 'We got money to burn.'

'That's five less for you,' Frank said, taking a pencil and notebook from his pocket. He pondered his figures. 'This is how I work it out. There's seven of you boys, what I might call our back-up, our foot soldiers. I'm gonna give you five hundred each. Seven by five hundred, that's three thousand five hundred. Agreed?'

'Yuh,' Abel drooled, his tongue hanging out. 'Suits me.'

Normally, Frank would have fobbed these smaller fry off with a hundred dollars and they would have been happy. To them it was a lot of money. But, as they were there at the count, he had to be honest with them.

'And I'm going to give a thousand dollars each to them I might term my lieutenants, Will, Sim, Clint, Miles, Charlie and Mike. OK?'

Those named grunted assent. 'Fair enough.'

'That leaves four thousand five hundred dollars. As your leader, my take's two thousand five hundred. And the rest goes to the man who gave us the information, soldier boy Jimmy here. May his platoon never catch up with him. Anybody any complaints?'

'Duh, no.' Abel reached a hand out. 'I'd like mine in silver coin, Mustuh Reno, that's OK with you. Don't like dis paper money.'

'Hold it right there,' Dunlap snarled. 'Two thousand? I didn't set this up for two thousand. I'm due to half what's here. You boys can split the rest whichever way you want. I'm due to seven thousand dollars, Frank.' He backed up against the door, levering his carbine. 'So you better start counting. Then I'm moving out of here.'

Frank's penetrating gaze met the soldier's, and he gave a thin smile. 'I'd advise you not to get greedy, Mister Dunlap. OK, I'll give you another five hundred of mine. That's two thousand five hundred. More than you deserve. So put that gun away and calm down.'

'You ain't fobbin' me off like that. What did these saddle trash do to deserve five hundred? Or your damn brothers? Cut their share and — '

Dunlap cleared his throat as smoke began to billow from the fire and fill the room and the boys started coughing. 'What the hell's going on?'

'You men in there,' a clear voice sounded from outside. 'We got you surrounded. Throw your weapons out. You'll step out with your hands high if you know what's healthy.'

'Jeesis!' Frank cried, flapping the smoke from his watering eyes. 'They've stuffed a coat down the chimney while we've been snapping at each other like coonhounds. Damn them.'

It was true. One of the possemen had sneaked up, hauled himself onto the roof and blocked the chimney. Now they were busy cutting dry sage in bundles, setting it alight and tossing it down against the windowless cabin walls. 'We'll burn you alive if you don't come out of there,' one shouted.

'I ain't givin' up,' Dunlap shouted, grabbing at the notes and stuffing them in his pocket. 'I'm fighting my way outa here.'

'You ain't got a chance,' Frank croaked back. 'They'll cut you to ribbons. But go ahead, see if I care.'

'Aw, hell,' Dunlap groaned.

'We're coming out,' Frank shouted, opening the door and tossing out his Smith and Wesson and Winchester. 'Hold your fire. Here I come.' He dodged out with his hands high and scuttled through the smoke.

A ring of stern-faced men greeted him, their rifles levelled, their fingers itching on their triggers. One frisked him. 'You tryin' to fool us,' he asked, finding the derringer. He grinned, dropped a lasso around Frank's shoulders and yanked it tight. 'You given us quite a ride.'

The others came scurrying out and were similarly trussed, and Dunlap, finally, showed himself, throwing his carbine out, angrily, and surrendering his cash. 'I worked hard for this,' he growled.

'Well, if it ain't Jimmy Dunlap. We been looking for you a long time,' a tall man, in range clothes, shouted. 'Who are these other monkeys? Ain't seen them in these parts afore.'

'We're drovers down on our luck,' Frank said. 'We should never have got mixed up in this fool scheme. He talked us into it.'

'A pity you didn't put up any resistance. We coulda cut you to pieces. We like a little duck shoot.'

'We're peaceful, law-abiding men by choice. We sure see the error of our ways. You'll find all the cash intact. If you boys could see your way to letting us go we would promise not to err again.'

'Dry your crocodile tears, friend. I'm Sheriff Marion of Magnolia. It's my duty to take you in. These boys happened to be herding some cows into town and came along for the chase.'

The tall sheriff collected up the silver and notes and swung into his saddle. 'Council Bluffs ain't so far off. We'll take you in there for tonight.'

'My stallion's lame.'

'So ride two-up. Or maybe you'd like to run behind?'

'That's a hundred-dollar horse. I sure don't like to leave him.'

'I'll pick him up sometime,' the sheriff said. 'I'm due to somethang out of this.'

* * *

Council Bluffs was a busy town, on the other side of the Missouri river to Omaha and on the main route of the cross-continental railroad west. Its jailhouse was a solid edifice made of rocks and cement with a log roof, but on the small side, just a sheriff's office, tucked in to one side, and a pen with floor to ceiling iron bars. When the fifteen outlaws were shoved into this there wasn't a lot of room to move.

'Hey, there's only two bunks,' Clinton moaned. 'Where do we get to stretch out?'

'You don't. And you don't get no food, neither, so shut up,' the Council Bluffs lawman, Marvin Brown, told them. 'You got a bucket to piss in. That's all you get.'

'You got any manacles for 'em?'

'Nope. We only got this here one ball and chain. We ain't used to accommodating crowds. Who shall I put this on?'

'That dingo Dunlap. He's the meanest, thievingest, slipperiest customer around. Wanted for desertion, murder, blackmail and rape.'

'Who are the others?' Marvin Brown asked, as the shackles were hammered onto the ankle of Dunlap, with the heavy chain and iron ball attached.

'Just small fry.'

'There,' Brown grunted. 'He won't get far in that.' He presented the ball to Dunlap and pushed him into the cage with the others. 'Sleep well, boys.'

'Solid as damn rock,' Clint muttered, as he grasped the thick bars. 'No way we're getting out through these. This is worse than the black hole of Calcutta.'

'Quiet,' Frank hissed. He was listening to what the lawman around the corner had to say.

It seemed like a Council Bluffs deputy named Bob had arrived to sit watch through the night. 'We've had a wire from some Pinkerton agents, Marv,' he was saying. 'They're on their way to identify them others.'

'They didn't say who they were?'

'No, they'll be looking to keep any reward money to themselves.'

'Well, we've had a hard, long day,' Sheriff Marion said. 'I'm cold, hungry and tired, so I'll join the men over at the saloon for some vittles and whiskey.'

'You can all bed down there on the floor,' Marvin told him. 'Bob here will keep an eye on thangs.'

'Can I leave this stolen cash in your office safe?' Marion asked.

'Sure, it'll be safe as houses with Bob.'

They heard a banging of doors and a turning of locks, and it fell silent.

'Hey, Deputy,' Dunlap called. 'How about some blankets in here? Some coffee? At least a bucket of water?'

The deputy showed himself from around the corner, but stood well back. 'You ain't gettin' nuthin' and I ain't unlockin' that cage, no way. I know your kind's monkey tricks. So shut up.'

He went back to his alcove to put his

boots up on the desk, and Trick Reno sighed, 'Ah, well, I guess I knew they'd catch us one day. A pity we didn't get to spend that money. Move over, fellas. I ain't even got room to breathe.'

They sat around, grunting and grumbling, for a while. There was no window in the cell and it soon began to whiff of unwashed body odours. 'Look at this,' Clinton whispered. He had been scraping with one of his spurs at the base of one of the rocks in the thick wall. 'Maybe we can get it loose.'

'You're wasting your time, kid,' Dunlap said. 'It would take all week.'

Frank stooped down and tried the rock, trying to get his fingernails into it. He shook his head. 'I don't know,' he hissed. 'You boys, back up against the bars. Block his view and start singing.'

'Singin'?' Abel looked dumbfounded. 'What we gonna sing?'

'Yeah, let's have a sing-song,' William urged. 'Ain't nuthin' else to do. How about, 'When we were marching through Georgia?'

'Good,' Frank said. 'Sing up, real loud. Come here, Dunlap.' He pulled the ex-soldier close and picked up his heavy ball and chain. He began swinging it and bashing it against the wall. Hard, harder.

'Ow, that hurts,' Dunlap yelped.

'Shut up.' Frank judged his swing and crashed the ball again. The rock shuddered. 'It's moving.'

'Let me try,' Clinton said. 'I got more weight than you.'

'Hoorah, hoorah, we sing in jubilee. Hoorah, hoorah, from Atlanta to the sea.' The men grinned as they sang at the top of their voices. 'When we go marching through George-gee-yah!'

'What in tarnation's going on?' The deputy appeared, with his newspaper in his hands. 'What a horrible cacophony. Cut it out will ya?'

The men kept on singing, as Clinton ceased hammering, momentarily. Bob scowled. 'Dunkheads.' And went back to his reading.

They took it in turns to hammer at the wall, the human shield of singers fast running out of words to their songs. They began to get a bit repetitive. 'How's it going?' Trick asked. 'I don't know no more tunes.'

' 'Sing The Land of Cotton'.'

'Thass a Reb song.'

'Just damn sing it. We're nearly through.'

'When I was in the land of cotton . . . '

Sure enough, the rocks had begun to crumble and fall away. Frank poked his head through the hole. The lane behind the jail, fortunately, was deserted. He could see the lights of the town, hear a piano tinkling, and down by the river a steam-boat blasted its steam horn. He wriggled on through. He looked about him, brushing himself down. Clinton had bashed the hole wider and stuck his head through.

'Come on,' Frank said. 'Tell the others to wait there. I got an idea.'

He walked around to the jailhouse

door, hammered on it, and shouted out, 'Open up, Bob. I brought you a beer.'

'Who's there?' a voice replied.

'It's me, Marv.' Frank muffled his voice with his hand. 'There's something I forgot. Get this door open. I brought ya some vittles.

'Just a second.' A key turned in the lock, and Bob's face appeared. He had a gun in his hand, but he didn't have time to use it before Clinton's fist smashed into his jaw. 'Unh,' was all he grunted as he collapsed on the floor.

Frank took his keys, his gun, the cash from the safe, unlocked for the others. He returned to the office, calmly counted out the promised cash to each of his men. 'Right, get going,' he said, after they had bound and gagged the deputy. 'It's best we split up. Good luck. See you back in Seymour. I believe you'll find your horses in the corral along the street.'

'Where are *you* going?' Abel asked.

'With my brothers. Get going, I said, 'fore somebody notices something fishy.'

They giggled and slipped away into the darkness.

'Where's mine?' Dunlap demanded.

'You don't get none.' Frank put the keys in his pocket. 'It wouldn't be no good to you. You ain't a hope of going nowhere with that ball and chain to carry.'

'You cheatin' bastard. Unlock this chain.' He tried to grab at Frank but Clinton hurled him back, his ball rolling after him. He tumbled him back in the cell and locked him in.

'So long, Jim. You shouldn't have gotten so greedy.'

Frank and the boys stepped outside, locked the door, and laughed, slapping at each other. 'Hey, it sounds like that steamboat's heading down river. Let's make a run for it.'

★ ★ ★

When Sheriffs Marion and Brown, with three Pinkerton agents, who had travelled all night to join them, went over early next morning to the jailhouse they found it locked. Round the back was a hole in the wall with the words chalked over it, 'April Fool!' It was April 1st, 1868.

'Shee-it!' Kilpatrick said. 'We come all this way for nothing again.' The horses had been scattered, and the only escapee they caught up with was Jim Dunlap hopping along ten miles out of town with his ball and chain in his hands.

9

The honest citizens of Seymour did not put out the welcome mat for the return of the Renos. Since they had been away the past fall and winter life had returned to normalcy in the little railroad town, and most folks hoped they had seen the last of them. But here they were back from Iowa with stolen silver in their pockets and greenbacks in their wallets. They set up their headquarters in the Red Garter saloon, and it was riotous business as usual. Saloon-keeper, Henry Holt, set the whiskey tap running and roulette wheel spinning, and stroked his 'danglers', the droopy ends of his moustache, one of the few glad to see them back. That was until Frank told him he was buying him out, lock, stock and barrel, for five hundred dollars, but he could stay and be bar-keep, if he liked.

'That's ridiculous,' Holt protested. 'What if I don't want to sell? I mean, I'm not going to. I've built this house up. It's mine.'

'He says, 'What if?' ' Frank eased the Smith and Wesson from its holster, his mad-looking eyes fixed on Henry. 'What is he going to do?' He threw five hundred dollars down. 'If I were him I'd go get my deeds outa the strongbox and hand 'em over, pronto.'

Frank had decided there was more profit in running a gaming house than being a customer in one, and the same went for running a whore-house. Why should Holt scoop off the cream?

He lost no time in re-recruiting his squirrelshooters and backwoods trash, and they sat around on the porch outside the saloon jeering at passers-by and full of their own importance. Frank wasn't over-enamoured of them, but he figured he needed protection in case of another posse raid, or if the Pinkerton boys tried to snatch him the way they had Big John.

He moved in, too, with Hetty, without a by-your-leave, as if he had never been away. 'I don't want you here, Frank,' she told him. 'I bought this cottage from the cash I made by my own honest industry, my sewing fingers. It's mine, its not yours. You haven't honoured a single promise you made me — '

He laughed, and tipped the contents of his saddle-bags out onto the bed. 'Look, that's all I got. A few thousand dollars. That ain't enough to set us up. I'm gonna marry you, Hetty, soon as I hit it big.'

'That's what you always say. Well, maybe I don't want you to marry me no more.'

'Come on.' He caught hold of her and pressed his face to hers. 'You know you missed me, same as I missed you. God, how I missed you, girl! We got that old magic together, you know that.'

Frank could be very persuasive when he wanted, and Hetty sighed, but submitted to his embraces. He was the only man she had known, physically, and she felt in a way as if she belonged to him. Frank vowed that all he wanted to do was go somewhere they weren't known, settle down, raise a family . . .

One of the first men he went to see once he was back in Seymour was Hank Diprose. 'Any news?'

'Yep. That five hundred of your'n I spread around has come up trumps.' The railroad clerk gave him a wink. 'There's a big consignment coming through next week. I'm pretty sure of that. The thing for you to do, Mr Reno, is hit quick 'fore the railroad bosses realize you're back.'

'Back in the railroad business, you mean?' Frank smiled, giving him a cigar.

His brothers and his gang members were told to get themselves ready for action. Abel Finnegan and a couple of cronies, Dick Coyle, in his greasy, fringed leathers, and Treat Gallagher, who smelt like the swamp rat he was, swaggered into the gunshop. 'We need the best revolver you got,' Abel said.

Harry Henshaw opened the glass case on his counter. 'Here you are, gents, the Allen and Hopkins, nickel plated .44 revolver, same calibre as your carbine to save carrying two types of ammo. Beautifully turned, six-inch barrel for quicker draw, mother-of-pearl grip. Top of the range at fifty dollars.'

'That's durn pricey, ain't it?' Coyle said, spinning the revolver on his finger, trying the hammer.

'Perhaps this is more for you? Colt army revolver, once the old cap and ball muzzle-loader kind. Now a Thuer conversion, bored through with a six-shot cylinder using .44 rimfire ammo. Just as good. Solid and reliable. Yours for ten dollars.'

'Yeah, this feels good,' Coyle grinned.

'You can have that,' Abel whined in his high-pitched voice. 'But I'm taking the fifty-dollar one and a box of forty cartridges, if you please, suh.'

'Glad to do business. You'll take them two? How about the other gent? I see he's got a revolver in his belt. What's that, the old Texas Paterson? May I see?'

'Duh? Yuh.' Treat handed the Paterson across. 'I got it from the white-haired agent who came nosing around. We had to do him over.'

'Ah, yes. One of the best. Looks like it was altered according to the Captain Farley plan. Ten-inch barrel. You don't see many of these around. Look after it, son, and it will look after you. Could do with some oil. May I sell you a bottle, fifty cents?'

The three men pocketed their purchases and began to leave. 'Just a minute. That's seventy dollars fifty cents you owe me.'

'We'll have to.' Abel grinned green, gappy teeth. 'We'll pay you when we done the raid.'

'But . . . ' Henshaw stood there open-mouthed in his apron. What could he do? He was one man against three of them. And the rest. 'This is barefaced robbery.'

What raid, he wondered, were they talking about?

★ ★ ★

Seymour was a small halt on the main north-south railroad. It had been used as a stopping point for taking on wood and water, but since the Renos had taken over the town most locomotives went rattling and whistling through as fast as they could without even slowing down. Those heading north were mostly goods vans packed with Texas longhorns destined for the Chicago slaughter houses. But, Frank Reno reasoned, those heading south were bound at some time to be carrying large amounts of cash, or, at least, bonds that his friend, Pete McCartney, could easily forge signatures to. The South was in ruins and the government was spending vast amounts on its reconstruction programme. Railroads and cities were being rebuilt. The workers, the army had to be paid, the materials bought. And, as Confederate currency was just worthless paper now, the bills had to be sent down from the north. So, Frank was hopeful that this tip-off might prove fruitful. Only a few weeks had passed since their Harrison County Bank heist. It was early May. The railroaders wouldn't be ready for this surprise attack. Or, at least, that's what he hoped. However, he took along a large body of his men, just in case.

'That sounds like the Whistling Billy on its way,' Billy Biggers yelled, as they heard the wailing 'whoo-whooing' of the steam whistle, and the faint clanging of its bell.

'You ready, boys?' Frank called. 'Remember, keep control of your trigger fingers. We don't want nobody killed.'

This time they had concealed themselves in wooded flatland to the south of Seymour, and, so that any guards on the train wouldn't get any warning, were trying a new mode of attack.

'He's gotten up a purty good head of steam,' William Reno gritted out, pulling his low-crowned hat down over his brow, and getting ready to give his Morgan the spurs. 'You figure we can catch him?'

'You're the ones who's catching him,' Clinton grinned, for the lighter and wirier of the Renos, Simeon and William, were the ones deputed to board the train. 'I'm just here to pick up your hosses.'

'Yeah, you would draw the easy straw,' Simeon growled, as he took his hat band between his teeth and held his reins in readiness. 'Sometimes I think you were born under a lucky star.'

The Jefferson, Missouri and Indianapolis locomotive was approaching along the arrow-straight track at a good lick, a white trail of woodsmoke pumping from its stack.

'Quit jabbering, boys, and let's go,' Frank yelled, moving his powerful horse out onto the hard track that ran alongside the railroad. He pricked the stallion's sides, a Smith and Wesson clutched in one hand, and headed away in the lead before the big locomotive, with its lamp and cowcatcher on the front, reached them. Soon the Morgan's muscles were pumping away in perfect balance, his big chest heaving, mane and tail flying, at full gallop, and Frank knew that they were a match for the train. In fact, he had to ease the pressure so it could come up alongside him. He saw the startled face of the engineer, in his goggles, peering across, and he cracked out a shot over his head.

Whooping like rebels the riff-raff in his gang had set off after him, riding along both sides of the train, firing their rifles and revolvers in a noisy concatenation of explosions to frighten any passengers who might have thoughts of resistance.

William and Simeon rode just behind Frank, Will judging his pace, waiting his chance, drawing alongside the open tender, loosing his stirrups, and — now! — hurling himself into space from the saddle to grab at the iron handles on either side of the open doorway, hauling himself aboard. One second of misjudgement, one slip, and he might well have been chopped to pieces by the churning wheels. But, no, he had made it. He grinned at the driver and fireman, pulling out his .45. 'Howdy, boys!'

Sim, behind him, had drawn alongside the wood tender, and, employing the same tactics, leaped to grab hold of its sides, his legs kicking in space, pulling himself bodily upwards, to scramble onto the pile of logs. He, too, gave a whistle of relief as he looked down at the ground flashing past. He pulled his Navy Colt from his holster, cocking it, climbing forward, and looked down at his brother in the cab with the two greasy-faced employees. 'How ya doin'?'

They weren't about to put up a

struggle. They were doing as they were told. The fireman had stepped to one side and the engineer was hauling on the brake. The wheels clamped in a shower of sparks and the train began to slide along the rails to a shuddering halt.

Meanwhile, at the rear of the train, Abel and Dick Coyce had swung from their horses onto the caboose platform as they galloped alongside, giving wild yells of triumph.

When the locomotive suddenly slammed on its anchors they were hurled forward through a door-way and found themselves in the guard's van, and a middle-aged man named Jesse Bean, who lived in Seymour, was facing them with a twelve-gauge shotgun in his hands. And from the look on his face they knew he was going to loose off a blast, which he did, but the sudden slowing in motion sent him awry, too, and the buckshot went wild over their heads.

Abel Finnegan didn't wait for him

to level the second barrel. His new Hopkins and Allen was in his fist, cocked and ready for use. He pumped out a slug that tore into Bean's chest, knocking him to the floor.

'Aw, shit,' Abel said, as he saw the blood begin to leak through the conductor's shirt. 'Frank ain't gonna be pleased about this.'

'You did it,' Coyce said. 'It weren't nuthin' to do with me.'

'Durn ungrateful fool,' Abel whined. 'I had to. He'd have kilt us both. You remember to tell that to Frank.'

He went over to the conductor and retrieved the fallen shotgun. 'Durn idjit,' he snarled, giving him a kick. 'What you go shootin' at us fer?'

There were two other railroad guards inside the baggage car, but when Abel poked his Allen and Hopkins through the barred airhole and shouted, 'I done fer Conductor Bean an' it's gonna be your turn next 'less you open up,' they decided to comply. All the noise of the shooting had made them nervous. They were not Pinkerton men, but uniformed employees, and they handed over their revolvers with hardly a murmur.

When Frank climbed up into the car they were already opening the safe. 'Good for you, Abel,' he said. 'Now let's see what they got.'

Even he was shocked by what he saw inside the safe. It was stacked with piles of notes, sacks of twenty-dollar eagles and silver coin. He swallowed and stared. 'Jess-is Ker-rist!' he whispered. He closed the door so that Abel didn't see too much. 'Get my brothers along here and tell Clint to bring them spare horses up. Dick, you take care of these two men. Take 'em down off the track and keep 'em covered. OK? What you waitin' for?'

'It weren't nothin' to do with me, Mister Reno.'

'What weren't?'

'Abel shot him, not me.'

'You evil, snake-tongued demon. Call yourself my friend? I had to shoot him, Frank. It was self-defence.

163

He fired his scatter-gun.'

'What?' Frank stood up, his dark eyes fierce. 'Is he dead?'

'No, Frank. He's just hurt. He'll pull through. Least, I think he will.'

'You fool. How many times have I told you? You should have knee-capped him.' He caught Abel by his coat and hammered a fist into his jaw, sending him sprawling to the floor. 'Get up. I'm gonna kick the shit out of you.'

'It was his own fault, Frank. It's that silly ole fool, Bean, got a house in Seymour. He shouldn't have shot at us. Who cares about him?'

'I do,' Frank roared. 'I do. This makes this a hanging offence. We ain't just robbers now.'

'What's going on?' Simeon asked, as he joined them. 'Simmer down, Frank. What's he done?'

'Go see if you can do anything for Jesse Bean. He's got a slug in him. Will, get your sacks ready. Abel, get out of here. I don't want to see your face around.'

'But you owe me. What about my share?'

'Get out.'

When he had gone, Frank turned to William. 'This is the biggest haul ever. I'm going to make a rough count. You start packing it away.'

Outside, the armed men on horseback were ordering the passengers out of the coaches, while inside the passengers were hurriedly trying to secrete valuables. Men pulled off boots and stuffed bankrolls inside. Women hurriedly unclipped necklaces, gold fob watches, keepsakes and brooches, and tried to hide them under the seat cushions of the Pullman car. Abandoning all modesty one hoicked her skirts up and thrust her reticule into her drawers, unaware that the Reno gang had little respect for womanhood, and could scent gold pieces like tracker dogs.

One elderly lady started to faint and fan herself, then, quickly recovered and ran out to the restaurant car kitchen, popping her handbag into one of the big pans. When Abel, intent on getting something for his trouble, came stomping through the cars, threatening men with his revolver, smacking one or two in the face to hurry them along, the woman offered him a few dollars from her purse.

'Why, thank you, lady. Now, where's the rest?' He put the Hopkins to her temple. 'I kilt one man awready today. It don't bother me to kill a female.' Screaming and shuddering, she led him to the kitchen.

Outside, the poorer folk, from the second-class coaches, were being lined up along the track and frisked, their valuables tossed in a sack. 'Thass all I got in the whole wide world,' a ragged-looking farmer complained, surrendering his cheap silver watch and worn wallet.

Trick Reno flicked it open, took a couple of bills. 'Aw, keep the rest, Grandad,' he said.

Back in the baggage car Frank was almost through counting. He could hardly believe it. 'I make it near on ninety thousand dollars.'

'Ninety thousand?' Will and Simeon stared at each other, speechless. Will gulped and gasped out, 'Now we really have got money to burn.'

'We'll hang onto most of this. So keep your mouths shut.' Frank began stuffing the silver into a carpet bag. 'Sling that over a hoss. And let's git outa here.'

'Ninety thou,' William muttered to Simeon. 'That's more than I ever heard of anybody having. The James gang never done anything near like this. They're amateurs compared to us.'

Frank, before he left, went to take a look at Conductor Bean. 'Howja feel, Jesse?'

'Aw, not so bad. Your brother done patch me up. I think it's missed my vitals.' He was groaning and straining for breath. 'I was a fool to fire at Abel.'

'You were, Jesse. You, indeed, were. Here, take this.' He pushed a roll of bills, one hundred dollars, into Bean's uniform pocket. 'You gonna need it for the doctor's bills.'

'Gee, thanks, Mr Reno,' Jesse wheezed. 'I guess it's yours to give away now.'

'It sure is.' Frank turned on his heel and jumped down from the caboose. Clinton had his horse collected and waiting. Frank put a boot in the bentwood stirrup and swung aboard. He rode along to see how the men were getting on. 'We'll have the share-out in two days time where I told you,' he shouted at them. 'So long.'

He and his brothers, Charlie Spencer, and another trusted cohort, Chuck Anderson, charged their horses away through woodland, leaping a wormwood fence, and ploughing across a field full of shimmering green spring wheat. The cold snap had passed, the sun was shining in a bright blue sky full of fleecy clouds, and, as they reached a trail of white dust, they passed a farmstead set amid cherry orchards, their branches ablaze with blossom.

'Boys, ain't life beautiful?' Frank shouted. 'That's the sort of place I'd like to buy for me and Hetty.'

'You can do now.' Charlie's walnutty, sideburned face grinned across at him. 'We're rich. I reckon we all can.'

'What we want a durn farm for? It ain't nuthin' but work,' Simeon shouted across, as they headed back towards Seymour. 'All I wants a bottle of hookus juice right now and a plump young whore in my arms.'

'You two, you wouldn't know where to put it,' Clinton jeered at them. 'You ain't never had a gal in your lives. Me, I'm gonna get measured for a heather tweed suit, with a diamond stickpin, and a gold-knobbed cane. A soak in a hot tub, and a touch of that French parfoom. That's the way to get the gals. They like you smellin' sweet, not like you two polecats.'

Frank didn't say any more. He was in a hurry to get back to Seymour and Hetty. She was the only gal he wanted.

She had been a bit cold and distant of late. Surely this — this fortune in his saddle-bags — would brighten her up? And then he thought of Jesse Bean and the day didn't seem quite so bright. He wondered what his brother in jail would think when he read about it. 'Thou shalt not kill.' That was big John's constant command. Frank shuddered as the thought of a hempen necktie crossed his mind. If anything happened to Jesse they would hold him responsible. Maybe now was the time to get out.

10

The bright days of April and early May had been a false spring, and the citizens of Seymour woke in mid-May to snow falling, and a wind swirling it into a spray of gritty ice. All day the sun was blotted out and it was almost as dark as night. If anybody had been watching Major McLaury's farm, with its rebuilt barns, they might have seen half a dozen furtive-looking men make their way there singly before nightfall.

'Are we all gathered here now, do you think?' the major asked, as his sister, Miss Sarah, served hot rum toddies to those assembled in their dining room.

'All them that's likely to come, I think, sir,' Hyram Jones replied. 'But maybe more will join us once the word gets round.'

'We're all agreed drastic steps are

needed, steps that would not normally be used, if we are to try to put a stop to the unlawful disorder and anarchy in this area?'

'If the law won't help us,' Doc Dooley said, 'we're forced to take matters into our own hands. We should see ourselves as surgeons who cut out the disease so the healthy body may live.'

'I will leave you to your discussion,' Miss Sarah said, and went out closing the door.

'The doctor's right,' gunsmith Henshaw agreed. 'These thieving pillagers got to be cut out from decent society. They owe me seventy dollars.'

'We should not be swayed by our own grievances,' the major advised. 'We will have to act with cold hearts, but fair ones, for the common good. How about you gentlemen?'

The sheriff of New Albany, Tom Stone, had donned a ragged fur coat, his big-boned face ruddy from cold riding. He leaned on a carbine and had a brace of revolvers in his belt.

'I've come because that lump of lard, Abe Wappenshaw, they jokingly call a sheriff, is less than useless to man or beast, and somebody's got to help you people out. You're getting no support from the army, or Washington, and you're more or less cut off. The Renos are riding roughshod over you all. The only ones doing anything are the rail-road police, that is, the Pinkerton agency, who have the contract, and even they seem helpless. I've already, as you know, tried to help them, raised a posse, led an attack with disastrous results. I can't do that again, even if I could raise the men, because I've been told Seymour is outside my jurisdiction. In fact, I've been slapped down by the New Albany council, but I ain't one to stand by and watch you suffer.'

'More succinctly, Mr Stone, you're with us?'

'That's right. The Renos ain't killed before, at least, as far as we can prove, but now a guard's been shot, Jesse Bean, who we all know as a man with a large family, nine kids in all, and it looks to me like he'll never work again. I hold the Renos responsible for that.'

'You're a lawman but you're willing to subvert the law to see the law reinforced?'

'I am. There ain't no question of honour when you're dealing with men like these.'

'It's a dirty business,' Major McLaury said. 'Not one I or you would ever have wanted to dirty our hands with. Even decent people will say we have no right to try to take the law into our own hands. And I say *try*, because there is no indication as yet that we may succeed. We are up against a ruthless pack of wolves. Quite simply we've got to try to defend the sheep, those among our community who are threatened, harried, stolen from, beaten, bullied, or put into a state of terror by these wolves. How about you, sir, would you agree?'

He was addressing the one who had yet to speak. Reuben Levitsky was a Jew in his twenties, darkly bearded and neatly dressed, who had set up a law practice in the district. 'I agree,' he said. 'I am a great believer in the law, both religious and governmental. I have seen the Renos flout it, impose their own law, that of threat, whippings and arson. I agree with you all. Something has to be done. And I am prepared to go to the ultimate.'

'Good. Then we are all agreed.' The major picked up his family Bible and passed it to Tom Stone. 'I want us all to swear a solemn oath that we, the Vigilance Committee of this county, known only to each other, vow to maintain this secrecy for all our days, to act in unison against wrongdoers, and to impose the ultimate punishment, if we all agree it necessary.'

'I vow to that,' Tom Stone said.

'Do you swear by your sacred honour to act as one, abiding by the majority vote, to reveal no secrets, and never desert each other or our standard of justice, so help you, in the name of God?'

'I do,' Tom said, passing the Bible on.

* * *

Frank Reno was still in a state of high excitement when he called on Hetty. 'Guess how much we took!' he shouted, as he burst into her cottage. 'Ninety thousand dollars! Nobody's ever robbed that much before. I've paid off my brothers and the men and I still got fifty thousand dollars left. Hetty, this is our dream come true.'

She glanced at him, but continued with her work. She did not seem very impressed. 'Really?' was all she said.

'Yes, really. What do you think of going north of the border, Hetty?'

'To Canada? Whatever for?'

'To live. They won't be able to get at me there.'

'Are you sure?'

'That's what I hear. We're rich, Hetty. We can buy a ranch up there, really live in style.'

He tipped the proceeds of the robbery on the bed, ran his fingers through the gold pieces and the notes, tossing them in the air. 'I gave the men five hundred dollars each, eight thousand each to Sim, Will and Clint, three thousand each to my lieutenants, and they were more than happy — you should hear them over at the saloon! And that leaves me fifty thousand dollars for myself, and expenses, a few railroadmen to pay off. With what I've already got we can live in clover, gal, for the rest of our lives.'

'Fifty thousand? That's an awful lot of cash.' Hetty was making last alterations to a long tweed skirt she was sewing, cut to flare like a trumpet, and she looked rather prim and proper with the pins in her mouth. 'I hear Jesse Bean got hurt.'

'Yeah, that fool Abel Finnegan. But

it was Jesse's fault for taking a pot at him.'

'Wasn't that his job to act as guard? He was only doing his honest duty.'

'Yeah, well, I'm sorry about Bean. I've seen him right. You know, I could hardly believe my eyes when I saw all that cash in the safe. This is the one we've been waiting for.'

Hetty didn't reply, but continued to tack at the skirt hanging from the tailor's dummy and the matching tweed jacket with its nipped-in waist. 'How do you like this design?' she asked. 'It's for one of *your girls*.'

Frank didn't like the way she said 'your girls'. A hint of disapproval. It was not as if he was rogering the silly little whores. He just collected the cash from the customers. 'You don't seem very thrilled by all this cash. I've done it for you, Hetty, for us.'

She bit her lower lip, bringing blood to its pale unpaintedness, and the gentle curve of her cheek was tense and unsmiling. She pretended to concentrate on her work. 'Perhaps a couple of tucks at the back.'

'For God's sake!' He knocked the dummy aside. 'I'm talking to you. You've no need to work your fingers to the bone any more, ruin your eyesight with all this sewing. What do you say?'

Hetty turned to face him and there were tears brimming in her eyes. 'I *like* my work, Frank. It is creative and honest. I am doing something worthwhile. What have *you* ever done, apart from steal?'

'What the hell's got into you? Why are you Miss Morality all of a sudden? Robbin' the railroad don't hurt nobody.'

'Apart from a hard-working fellow like Mr Bean, who has a large family dependent on him. What happens to them if he can't work no more?'

'I told you, I've looked after him. I gave him a hundred dollars.'

'A hundred dollars. Big deal. How long will that last with nine mouths to feed?'

'Don't give me this. I thought you'd be happy, at last. Once we get to Canada we can get hitched. We can have some kids. You know that's what you want.'

'Do I? And what if I'm left to bring them up on my own like Mrs Bean might well be?' Hetty had been worried enough about avoiding pregnancy. She had been using pessaries of coconut butter and quinine prescribed by Doc Dooley, but she was by no means sure that that was foolproof. Frank, of course, in his cavalier way, had refused to use any precautionary methods. He claimed that to wear a pig's gut sheath interfered with his pleasure. 'I would love to have a baby, if I thought it had the chance of being brought up in a happy and contented marital home.'

'This is your chance. Are you coming to Canada, or not?'

'They have very cold winters. Even worse than here.'

'Aw, come on. Where the hell do you want to go, Mexico?'

'I didn't say that.' Hetty righted the dummy and its clothes, poked at the log fire of the stove, and laid a cloth on the table. She lit a candle, for it was getting dark, and she did not much like the smell of the kerosene lamp. She filled a bowl with soup of asparagus, picked from her own garden, and placed a piece of homebaked pumpernickel bread alongside. 'Supper's ready,' she said.

Hetty was wearing a black velvet, wasp-waisted dress of her own design, with a big cowl collar laid flat across her shoulders to reveal her slender neck. She filled her own bowl with soup and sat down opposite Frank's place.

Suddenly he was standing behind her and his strong fingers were around her neck, looping something cold around her throat. 'Howja like this?' He clipped the necklace together and arranged it above her breasts. 'Real amethysts and opals.'

She looked down and the jewels on

the dark dress seemed like tears. 'Who did you steal it from?'

'For Chrissakes!' He clenched her shoulders. 'Sometimes I want to break your little neck. I *bought* it as a wedding present. I thought it might cheer you up. Ain't you pleased?'

'Yes, it's very nice. She stifled the desire to ask, 'With whose money?'

'Eat your soup, Frank, before it gets cold. You know I don't like you to blaspheme in my house. You can blaspheme all you like outside.'

'You're enough to make a man curse his own mother.' He usually said grace to humour her. But he began to eat in peeved silence, swabbing up the soup with his bread. 'Is this all there is?'

'No, there's rabbit pie in the oven.'

He wanted to tell her that the food was good, that she looked beautiful in the candlelight, but he couldn't utter the words. She had made him angry, sour and mean.

'You haven't answered me, about Canada.'

Hetty was silent for a while, avoiding his eyes. She said, quietly, 'I'll think about it.'

'OK, maybe it's best I go up and get settled, and send for you?'

'Maybe that's best.'

★ ★ ★

'Cigars and bourbon an' wild, wild wimmin,' Clinton grinned. 'They drivin' me crazy, they drivin' me insane.'

'That woman of mine sure is,' Frank said, grimly. He had left Hetty's soon after supper. He would have loved to have stayed and made love to her, but there wasn't much point with her in that mood. He wasn't going to beg, no way. 'You know that expensive necklace I bought her? She more or less accused me of stealing it. You would have thought she would have been grateful.'

'Wimmin,' Clinton drunkenly philosophized. 'You just can't please 'em. You should never have got serious,

Frank. Me, I like these sorta li'l gals. You pay for what you get. Or, I tell you what, other men's wives. Thass what I specialize in. That way I don't pay nuthin'. The husband pays for 'em. An' they're real grateful for all they get on the side. Some of them wives out in them backwoods, they're real hot.'

'Yeah, I'm sure. One of these days one of them husbands might be gettin' hot, too, with his hands around your collar, that is.'

'Aw, who cares?' Clinton reached for his bottle of bourbon. 'Forget your troubles, Frank. Have a drink.'

Frank forced a smile, although his anger with Hetty still smouldered. The boys had been having a high old time since he had paid them out. Wine, women and whiskey, like Clinton said — and stolen cash — was sending them all crazy. He might be forced to recruit more girl-power and keep the Red Garter open to the early hours. Still, what he had paid out to them would mostly be pumped back into his coffers. He couldn't lose!

When Frank had pushed through the bat-wing doors they had cheered and buzzed around him, vying to pat him on the back and buy him a drink. It was as if he were their saviour. They relied on him to lead them. 'When's the next hit, Frank?' they asked.

'Aw,' Frank smiled. 'Sooner or later.'

But he became more serious when talking to his brother.

'I'm getting out, Clinton. I've had enough. Hetty don't approve of my lifestyle and I don't blame her. If I want her to stay with me I've got to settle down and be an honest man. In a coupla days I'm headin' for Canada. And this time I won't be coming back. Hetty says it's too cold, but, hell, other folks don't mind it. Cold's healthy. Anyway, she'll come once she sees I'm serious.'

'But, ain't we gonna do any more hits?'

'Things are gettin' too hot around here. They're not going to let us get away with it. If you, Sim and Will have any sense, you'll come with me. But, it's up to you, you can please yourselves. Where are those two, anyway?'

'They've gone out to the ranch. The old man's injured hisself, didn't you hear? The silly ole fool. He was guiding a stallion into a mare and he got caught between the two of 'em. The times he's told us to beware!'

Frank smiled. It was ironic, really. All those years of breeding horses, and to get crushed like that. 'He's probably broke an arm or cracked a rib.'

He looked around at the scene of dissolute abandon in the saloon, his men packed at the bar slinging back whiskey and beer as if it might be the last day of their lives. Or gathered around the faro and roulette tables. The skimpily clad good-time gals were dancing the two-step, as a fiddler scraped and the piano-player jangled the ivories, and three painted hussies kicked their stocking-clad knees up, flashing their furbelows, on the rostrum. 'It seems a shame to leave this profitable establishment,' he said. 'Maybe I'll bequeath it to you, Clinton. It seems to be your element.'

'It certainly is,' Clinton howled, and staggered over to the dance floor, scooping up one of the under-age nymphs, and carrying her up to the bedrooms. He turned on the landing, a big grin on his face, a cigar stuck in his jaw, and hollered, 'Here's to the Renos!'

Frank smiled and went behind the bar to check the takings before sitting in on a game of poker that might well last until the next morning.

★ ★ ★

Bad news, however, came with sun-up. William and Simeon arrived on horseback with news that their father's injuries were worse than expected. He had been badly crushed by the weight of the stallion. In fact, he might well be on his deathbed. Frank had never been fond of his father. But it was his mother he thought of. She would need support at a time like this. He would have to postpone his journey to Canada.

Frank rode out to the ranch. The old patriarch was hardly able to talk, breathing hard. Some kind of internal bleeding. He just lay in his bed and glowered at him. It was strange to see him so helpless. His mother seemed so weakened by it, too.

'Satan sure finds work for idle hands,' was about all his father was able to cough out at him, in his disapproving way.

'Frank,' his mother begged. 'If you're going to lead the boys on any more of these robberies, don't take Clinton. We need one of you here to look after the place.'

'Sure, Ma, I promise,' he said, giving her a hug. 'I'll tell Clinton he's got to pull himself together. Anyhow, I ain't expecting to do any more jobs, I'm going away with Hetty.'

Three days later their father died.

They held the burial service at the ranch and he was interred in the family plot. 'You've sown your wild oats. It's time to knuckle down,' Frank told Clinton. 'Somebody's got to stay, look after Ma, and run this ranch, and you're the chosen one.'

'Hey, I ain't cut out for ranching, you know that.'

'Tell you what, why don't you take turns at running the saloon and the ranch? When you get tired of one, you go back to the other. But somebody's got to look after these Morgans. They're an important breed. And I'm relying on you. I may well be sending for some from Canada.'

'OK, Frank, you're the boss. And if it's what Ma wants.'

Frank, Will and Sim, climbed onto their thoroughbreds and left their mother kneeling at the grave in the cold wind, Clinton standing beside her. 'He'll look after her,' he said. 'He's solid as a rock underneath.'

Frank returned to Hetty's cottage.

She had sewn him a kind of canvas waistcoat, with long pockets stitched all around it, which he could wear under his shirt. He exchanged his gold coin for greenbacks at the saloon, and managed to stuff thirty thousand dollars in wads of notes into the pockets. The other twenty thousand he would carry in his saddle-bags. He didn't trust banks. They were liable to get robbed. Or go bust.

The three Renos were about ready to head for the border when Hank Diprose gave Frank another tip-off. 'The word is there's a consignment coming which will be almost as big as the last. It will be on The Flyer, heading through Seymour next week.'

Frank tugged at his goatee beard and glanced at his brothers. 'I ain't greedy,' he said. 'But this is too good to miss.'

11

They were standing on the wooden platform of the railroad station at the busy town of Columbus when The Flyer came chuffing and hissing and clanging in from Chicago. Frank Reno, in his wide-brimmed black hat, his caped greatcoat and clean linen, looked like any prosperous rancher, as, with Simeon and William, in their cowboy clothes, he waited among other passengers to board the train. There were three coaches, a couple of goods trucks, and at the rear a long armoured car. Beyond that was the conductor's caboose. Frank looked along the platform and saw six of his men mingling with the crowd. The Adams armoured car remained closed, so Frank muttered, 'Here we go.' And they all stepped aboard.

They had travelled up to Columbus,

the nearest big town north of Seymour. This seemed an easier way of stopping a train than chasing after it on horseback. It was early morning. Frank found a seat in the restaurant car, his brothers sitting opposite. It was warm, but he didn't want to take off his greatcoat and reveal the hardware beneath it, the ivory-handled Smith and Wesson and the sawn-off shotgun in the deep pocket inside his coat.

'How about some breakfast?' he said, raising a finger to a Negro waiter.

Hank Diprose had reported that a colleague had bust the railroad code. The Ohio and Mississippi Flyer would be carrying one hundred thousand dollars on this trip in their Adams Express Company car. There might, it was believed, be two or three guards inside. But with the Renos' thirty-man back-up there was nothing to worry about. Frank smiled confidently as the white-coated waiter poured coffee from a silver pot, and the bushes and trees and fields and scattered farm-houses moved by outside their window. Clouds of white smoke wafted past, they could hear the powerful pistons of the locomotive dragging them on towards — what? — but the warmth of the sun, the rattle of the wheels on the rails, clickety-clacketing, rhythmically, and the telegraph wire seeming to float up and down on its poles on the bank outside, imparted a hypnotic sense of security.

It seemed they had hardly finished their breakfast before they went whistling and screaming through Seymour, and Frank caught a glimpse of the Red Garter and Hetty's cottage. 'It's time,' he said, getting to his feet, consulting his watch.

Charlie Spencer and Trick Reno had appeared at the end of the packed restaurant car, holding carbines across their chests. 'Everybody stay where you are,' Charlie shouted, his forage cap pulled down over his brow, his dark, carved face severe. He had a touch of Cherokee blood in him. 'Nobody make a move. Nobody gets hurt. We want you to get your valuables ready to toss into this gunny sack we brought along.'

Frank and his brothers walked past them and through the doors, crossing the open-air 'bridge' to the next carriage. At the far end of this one were Chuck Anderson and Miles Ogle, carrying ready-cocked revolvers. Frank paused to make sure none of the passengers were going to give any trouble, and passed on through. In the next doorway he met the waiter, his eyes goggling at him, the cups on his tray rattling due to his shaking hands. 'Get back to your kitchen,' Frank said, 'and stay there. Wait a second, I ain't paid you, have I?' He passed him a ten-dollar note. 'I'm Frank Reno. Wish me luck.'

They left the Pullman area and entered the second-class car, with its rougher-looking travellers. But they, too, were staying quiet under the watchful eye and guns of Jesse Thompson and Billy Biggers. As he reached them, Frank turned and shouted, 'Listen, everybody. We're the Renos. We don't want to kill anybody, in fact, we pride ourselves we never have. But if we have to, we will do. Savvy? Just do what you're told and you'll be OK.'

He and his brothers went on through, and leapt across to the fuel tender as the iron wheels rattled by beneath them. They climbed up onto the logs. Simeon pulled a Colt revolver from the big carpet bag he was carrying, and a carbine. He gave the carbine to his brother and kept the Colt .45 for himself. They nodded to each other, as the wind ripped at their hats, and climbed forward across the logs behind Frank. The engineer and fireman raised their hands with surprise as Frank jumped down into the cab, and his brothers covered them.

Frank studied the countryside passing by, and shook his head. He consulted his watch again. Ah, now they were entering a low-lying area of swamp half-way to New Albany. 'Slam on the brakes!' he shouted.

There was the customary rattling and hissing and screeching as the locomotive came to a halt, and Frank saw his men waiting among the trees and their spare horses tied to a bough. He waved to them. 'Howdy, boys. Ain't we dead on time?'

The gang members gave a jubilant cheer and some came running towards Frank as he left Will to guard the cab, and jumped down. Among them was Abel Finnegan, wall-eyed and grinning foul teeth, his longarm slung over his back, his new Allen and Hopkins in one hand. 'You done it again, Frank!' he yelled.

The more cautious sat their horses, with double-bands of ammunition strung across their shoulders, watching for trouble. Wilder ones were firing into the air to frighten the folks in the coaches. But they too were glad to see their leader arrive, expecting a good pay-off, once more.

'Don't count your chickens before they're hatched, Abel,' Frank said, as he and Simeon went crunching along the gravel track accompanied by a bevy of backwoodsmen. 'We still got to get these guys to open up.'

'Aw, they won't give us no trouble.' Abel, in his coonskin cap, laughed and ran ahead, accompanied by Dick Coyce and the hare-lipped Treat Gallagher, intent on proving themselves. They reached the armoured car and Abel shouted up. 'Y'all in there! We're the Reno gang. Throw your weapons out and come out with your hands grabbin' air. Don't give us no trouble.'

This time the armoured car had a door in the side, the kind that was let down to allow horses to disembark. 'OK, boys,' a voice whined through the letterbox-like spy hole. 'Here's our guns.' A couple of Winchesters were thrust through the hole, and the hillbillies fought for possession of the prized arms. 'We're coming out.'

Frank and Simeon had been delayed by Charlie Spencer, who caught hold of Frank's arm and said he smelled a rat. 'There's a coupla guys in there ain't right. They had revolvers hid in their pockets. I figure them for Pinkerton men.'

Frank Reno didn't have a chance to reply for the door of the armoured car had crashed down and there was a volley of explosions. He saw Abel go hurtling back to land in the brackish water of the swamp. Dick Coyce fired his Navy, but up into the branches, because a slug had ploughed into his thigh and sent him hopping and tripping away. The skinny swamp rat Treat Gallagher was trying to aim his long-barrelled Paterson but it was too heavy for his thin wrists, and his shot was wasted, as a fusillade of lead poured from the armoured car and he, too, went down.

'Surprise, surprise!' Charlie Durango drawled as the ramp fell down and the array of hillbillies faced him. And the surprise was on their faces as he fired his twin Colt .45s point blank at them. There were screams as they fell back and tried to escape.

Behind Durango were Allan Pinkerton, Tom Patterson and Pat Kilpatrick, joining in the attack, sending snub-nosed bullets of high velocity pouring into the men who faced them. And with them were other gunmen Pinkerton had recruited to come along on this foray. His words had been, 'We're gonna clean out the Reno scum once and for all.' It had been easy to feed false information along the line. Instead of a car full of cash, the bandits would get a welcome of blazing lead.

Abel surfaced from the filthy water, spitting a spout of it out, a fierce pain pounding through his shoulder. He clambered to his feet, backpedalling, trying to fire his new nickel-plated revolver at the men on the train. 'Dang me!' he cried. 'What's the matter with this thang?' He did not realize he had to release the new-fangled safety-catch. He screamed and fell back as another bullet cut through his leg.

Frank Reno watched, heartstruck, for moments unable to move, or comprehend the situation. 'It's the Pinkertons,' he eventually shouted, waving to his mounted men to move in. 'Go get them boys. There ain't many of 'em.'

But there were more. And they were on the passenger train. Suddenly they sprang into action, pulling out concealed weapons, aiming at the men who were ordering people to bring out their valuables. Charlie Spencer was hit in the arm, firing back, as he retreated. Trick Reno caught hold of him round the body, ostensibly to help, but Spencer had the idea he was using him as a shield. Nonetheless they managed to scramble out of the train to find a full-scale shooting war going on.

Trick Reno, being a Reno, took to his heels. The Renos had a strongly inbuilt sense of self-preservation, what some might call a yellow streak, and Frank Reno was no exception. As he urged his men in to attack the visitors in the armoured car, he backed away, dragging Simeon with him, and ducked down under the carriages. From there they watched the gun-battle rage, the clouds of powder smoke rolling, the screams and shouts and explosions almost deafening.

'God knows how many men they got,' Frank growled into his brother's ear. 'But this ain't good news. The bastards tricked us. There ain't no cash. It's time to get outa here. Go get Will an' make a break for it.'

He patted Simeon on the back, pushed him out, and dodged back to the other side of the track where there wasn't so much happening. The boys watching that side of the rails weren't sure what was going on. 'We're being attacked,' he shouted. 'Git on the other side and give 'em a hand.'

Frank bumped into Charlie Spencer

as he stumbled from the train. 'Come on!' he shouted, dragging him towards some abandoned horses. 'It's time to get outa here. It's everyone for themselves.'

Frank did have the decency to help Charlie onto a horse, and then they set off back along the track, the sound of shooting and shouting ringing in their ears until it became just a faint sound. They reined in their horses to wheel them around, and listen. There was the thud of galloping hooves and Frank raised his Smith and Wesson in anticipation. But he recognized the leading rider, Miles Ogle, who shouted out, 'Don't shoot! It's us.' He was being followed by Albert Perkins and Mike Rogers. The hauled in, their eyes panicked.

'Come on, boys,' Frank said. 'I think it's all over. I think it's time we headed for Canady.'

12

Earlier that morning there had been an insistent banging on the door of Major McLaury's farmhouse. His sister, Sarah, opened to meet the frightened face of Henry Holt, former owner of the Seymour saloon, the activities therein she would not care to dwell upon. It had the reputation of being a regular Sodom and Gomorrah.

'Yes?' She was polite but reserved in her manner. 'Did you wish to speak to my brother?'

'I've come by the backroads,' Holt said, 'so nobody would see me.'

The major rose from his chair, a pipe in his mouth, and a quill pen in his hand, as Holt was shown into his study. He was writing his Civil War memoirs. 'Forgive me if I take a few seconds coming back to reality. I was in the middle of the Shenandoah campaign,' he said. 'Perhaps, Sarah, you would bring us coffee?'

'I've come, sir, to offer information. There's been a whisper that a Vigilante Committee's been formed. You being a leading citizen I thought you could, like, pass this information on. You see, I want you honest folks to know that I'm on your side. I don't want nothing to do with the Renos.'

'That's why you let them use your saloon as a headquarters, why you pander to them with poor, destitute girls, profit from their misfortune, supply whiskey at all hours to intoxicate the unworthies who gather in your establishment, and inflame them to cause mischief and mayhem throughout the night, so honest citizens rarely get a wink of sleep?'

'But, I don't sir. The Renos stole my establishment from me. It's them. They make me do it. I work as bottle-washer for a pittance. If I volunteer this information am I — ?'

'Of course, man. Good for you

for coming forward. You have our protection. Well, spit it out. I haven't got all day.'

'I heard 'em talking, sir. There's summat going on. Today. Down at the Potawtonki swamp. They all goin' to meet there. I reckon it's another railroad hit.'

'What time?'

'They said 'bout noon.'

'Good.' The major looked at his watch. He went out to the kitchen. 'Sarah, I want one of the farm boys to run a message to those people on my list. Tell him to simply say, 'Time to strike'.'

Two hours later, Major McLaury and his sworn-in committee, plus three newcomers, Fred South, a hog gelder, Tim Freemantle, a cattle merchant, whose cheques hadn't been getting through to the south, and Sam Spry, a housetiler, were riding fast south. They were all fully armed, if experienced mainly at hunting animals and vermin, not men. They rode into the swamp from the trail and missed by a whisker Frank Reno and his lieutenants riding hard up the railroad line.

★ ★ ★

Bullets had furrowed scalps, clipped earlobes, pierced calves, as the brief battle at the armoured car ensued. The ferocity of the attack by the Pinkerton men had put the fear of God up the Reno gang, unused to being on the receiving end of lead, and they had quickly panicked, once they realized their leaders had abandoned them. They had gone splashing through the swamp, or headed away in all directions.

Allan Pinkerton sent a few parting shots after those fleeing on horseback and on foot, and tried to calm the passengers on the train. 'Don't worry, folks,' he shouted. 'The Renos ain't used to talking to hot lead. They've turned tail like the cowards they are.'

In spite of all the flying lead, by

some miracle, the one that hung like a halo over the Reno boys, nobody had been killed. Plenty of the gunmen had received flesh-wounds, and one lady who had hid in the train lavatory had caught a bullet that smashed through the wooden-casing into her bare rump. But, apart from that, in the panic, shots had gone wild.

Five of the Renos' men, who caught the first fusillade, had been cut down, and were hauled out of the swamp groaning and cursing. 'This durn useless Hopkins,' Abel whined, brandishing it. 'Cost me fifty dollars. I been cheated. It won't shoot.'

'All we seem to have caught are the small fry,' Pinkerton said, giving a derisory look at Abel's injured buddies, Treat Gallagher and Dick Coyle. 'Ain't it odd how the big boys get away?'

Charlie Durango's mahogany face split into a grin. 'Waal, at least we put 'em on the run. I think we done OK.'

'Frank Reno and some of his boys

headed up towards Seymour,' Tom Patterson said. 'Hadn't we better get after them, Chief?'

'Good thinking. Come on, boys. Can we leave you here, Charlie, to calm down these passengers and send them on their way? And look after these prisoners until we get back?'

'Sure thang,' Charlie said, and watched as the Pinkerton men found abandoned horses and set off up the track. He turned to the five abject backwoods boys. 'Hey, where you get that Paterson?' he asked The Flyer's engineer.

'That feller with the hare-lip had it. I disarmed him.'

'That's my gun. Ain't I glad to see it back. You better be heading on, mistuh, to New Albany. Thanks for your help.'

As the train went shunting and puffing on its way, Charlie said, 'Shee-it! I shoulda loaded you all into the baggage car and taken you to the jail down there. Hot damn, what am I thinkin' of? Looks like y'all have to wait around for the next train.'

He sat on a rock and watched his unarmed prisoners. 'Jeez,' he said, rolling a cigarette. 'It's been quite a day.'

The prisoners were moaning and bewailing their fate, looking at their various wounds, which weren't life-endangering, when a couple of real swamp rats, two ragged men, barefoot, undersized, with sallow hatchet faces, silently arrived, poling a punt. 'We heard the shootin',' one said, stepping ashore. 'What's goin' on?'

Charlie Durango eyed the swamp rat askance, and the rifle he had under his arm. He said, 'The Reno gang. We've caught these varmints.'

'The Renos? One of them's been after my missis, sniffin' around while I was away huntin'. She tol' me. They don' deserve to live.'

'Hey, hold on,' Durango said, and his Paterson came out to cover the two evil-looking men. 'These men got a right to a fair trial. You ain't having 'em.'

'We don't know nuthin' about your missis,' Abel sneered. 'Thass probably that durn Clinton. He's been in the pants of near every woman in the neighbourhood, him and his cigars.'

There was another splashing sound and Charlie saw a dozen horsemen approaching along the side of the swamp through the trees, only there was something strange about them. They were all wearing sack-like masks over their heads, with slits for eyes.

'What'n hell?' Durango said, jumping back to point his revolver at them. 'Who'n hell are you?'

The strangers did not speak, just held in their horses, and took in the scene through their slit masks.

Durango was trying to cover them and at the same time keep an eye on the two river rats who were skulking around. He turned to aim his Paterson at them, but one of the masked men spoke.

'I wouldn't do that. It would be advisable if you dropped that gun.'

It was a cultured voice with an air of authority, and the rider speaking had a saddle gun trained on him in a very decisive manner. 'We are here on vigilance duty. We mean no harm to you. We advise you to go on your way.'

The swamp rats and horse riders had manoeuvred themselves around him, so there was nothing Charlie could do but surrender his gun. 'Aw, shee-it,' he groaned. 'You cain't do this. This ain't legal.'

'What you men wearin' them funny masks fer?' Abel asked, but there was a quiver of fear in his voice. 'You say you vigilantes? We ain't nuthin' to do with the Renos. It's them you want to go after. They headed back up to Seymour.'

'We are after all of you,' another of the masked men said, in a muffled, sepulchral voice. 'Small fry and big fry. We're going to clean you out like the vermin you are.'

'And I am afraid, my friends,' the cultivated voice said, 'we are starting with you.' He turned to his comrades. 'Are we all agreed? Shall we take a vote on it?'

'Ain't no need,' another masked man said. 'Let's get on with it.' He took a lariat from his saddle horn and spun it over a firm bough. He jumped from his horse and slipped the noose over Dick Coyle's head. Coyle screamed and tried to struggle away but two other hooded men had hold of him. 'Sit him on my hoss.'

'Fellas, what are you doing? This is preposterous.' Charlie Durango stared at them. 'These are my prisoners. You can't do this. They're due to a trial. This is murder.'

'We've given them a fair trial,' the leader said. 'We are the jury. We have agreed. The sentence is death.'

'No!' Coyle gurgled, as they lifted him onto the horse and tightened the end of the rope to a spur of the tree. He started crying. 'Please. I got fambly.'

'Too late for pleading.' It was an older man's reedy voice that spoke, and he slashed his quirt across the horse's backside. 'We have to cut you out like poison. Haagh!'

The horse started forward, and Coyle was left dangling and kicking air. The leader of the vigilantes raised a revolver and shot him as he hanged.

'Good,' one of the swamp rats said. 'Thet's one gawn. Now for these two.'

Charlie Durango swallowed, feeling like he was going to be sick, as he watched the other four, Abel Finnegan and Treat Gallagher, and two ill-formed unknown incompetents, hoisted, crying and begging, onto horses, and lynched. His ears rang as the vigilantes emptied their revolvers into their swinging bodies. He was left in the roil of powder smoke and watched them riding away.

'Yeah, you've done your Christian duty,' he yelled after them. 'You lousy bastards.'

He glanced up at the bodies twisting on their ropes, suddenly peaceful in their looks, picked up his Paterson and went to find a horse. 'Poor devils,' he said. 'they didn't give 'em a chance.'

The swamp men were picking up what abandoned arms they could find, pulling the boots from the hanging men. When he got back they had gone. 'Christ, this place gives me the creeps,' Charlie said. 'I wish I was back in Wyoming.'

13

Frank Reno only paused long enough when he reached Seymour to call at Hetty's cottage, grab his waistcoat and saddle-bags of fifty thousand dollars, say a brief goodbye — 'things gawn wrong; I'll send for you, gal' — rifle the safe at the Red Garter, and get fresh horses out at his mother's ranch. He, and his trusted cohort of five men, rode north, their spirited Morgans easily out-distancing the pursuing Pinkerton men.

Summer and fall passed and Frank put his wealth to good use, buying a fine spread in a secluded valley just north of the border. He had access to a lake and river, a wealth of grass surrounded by timberland teeming with game. The house he bought was like a castle compared to Hetty's cottage, built of brick and wood, with a fine stone fireplace and new double-thickness windows, a study, library and dining room, several bedrooms, and, outside, corrals, barns and bunkhouse. 'It is paradise here,' he wrote to Hetty. 'Winter is tightening its grip, but it will pass, and I'll send for you in the spring.'

Hetty knew that Frank, in his way, loved her, and she found his belief that all would be well now he had given up 'robbing' somehow touching. Inside she dreaded the days ticking the winter away. Come spring, she knew, she would have to go to him. She had promised to marry him. She was his woman. That's all there was to it, like it or not.

Allan Pinkerton had put all his many other cases on the back-burner. He had become obsessed with tracking the Renos down. For the moment Frank Reno was safe from the long arm of United States law in the haven of the British Dominion. Or so Allan believed, although he had no idea, as yet, of his whereabouts. He was not interested in the rank-and-file members of the gang. Most were no-account no-goods, not worth bothering with.

He would have liked to have arrested Clinton Reno, the youngest brother. But he had not been at the scene of the abortive rail hold-up — he had a foolproof alibi — and Pinkerton would find it hard to make a case stick that he had been along on the other raids. He had vacated the Red Garter saloon, and appeared to have 'found God', living a low-profile life of honest toil at his mother's horse ranch. Pinkerton decided to leave him alone.

The other two brothers were a different kettle of fish. While obviously minor partners, they had taken major roles in all the robberies. Pinkerton telegraphed his three faithful blood-hounds, Patterson, Kilpatrick and Durango, to track down William and Simeon Reno.

It was a long, arduous trail, following the spoor of dollars frivolously spent, out into the wilds of Missouri once more. It was late fall by the time they finally caught up with the boys in a whorehouse at Willow Springs. Will and Sim had taken Clinton's advice and were whooping it up with whiskey and cigars. Naked in bed with a couple of naughty girls they had not time to go for their guns. The Pinkerton agents took them back to New Albany and installed them in the two-storey jail to await their trail.

Meanwhile, Allan Pinkerton had been intercepting Clinton's and Hetty's mail. A letter to Hetty gave a full description of his ranch in Ontario — 'you'll love it here' — and instructions how to get there. At last! Pinkerton pondered the possibility of kidnapping Frank, perhaps doping him with chloroform and transporting him back across the border. But he wanted to do things legally, so he instituted extradition proceedings with Queen Victoria's representatives in Ontario. As always, the lawyers sliced the baloney thin, put up a smoke screen. No, impossible. Pinkerton pressed his suit, going through Washington. At last, he received the news he wanted. If Frank Reno had taken up Canadian citizenship it would have been no go. But, he was still an American subject, and a notorious train robber. An undesirable alien. Permission granted. Pinkerton headed north with his three agents.

★ ★ ★

Windsor, where he liaised with the Royal Canadian Mounted Police, was a wide-open, rumbustious border town, a false-fronted strip of saloons, dance halls, billiard parlours, stores and cat-houses, where an array of trappers, travellers, loggers and low-lifes gathered to spend their money on bad whiskey and worse women.

'I always had the idea Canada was a peaceful, law-abiding place,' Allan Pinkerton said, as they sat in a saloon amid its rowdy inmates.

'We've got our share of deadheads and desperadoes,' Sergeant Sam Farson replied, with a grim smile. 'A place like this is plagued with smugglers and criminals evading justice. Normally, we wouldn't have the time or manpower to pursue a man like Reno, particularly as he has committed no crime in this country.'

'So, why the change of heart?'

'The large scale of his robberies, your persistence, and, perhaps, the possibility that he might start robbing trains here if he gets low on funds.'

The sergeant was wearing winter garb of fur hat and greatcoat over his scarlet uniform jacket. He had four mounties under his command. Pinkerton had hoped for a larger outfit, unsure how many men Reno might have enlisted as protection. But he guessed this was all the help they were going to get. Ghost River, where the ranch was located, was a day or more away. So they lost no time and set off on their horses, the straight-backed mounties on their uncomfortable-looking English saddles, led through the snow by an Indian, Dan White Smoke.

They camped that night by a frozen lake. Dan had a fire going in no time, and acted as a cook, mixing flour with melted snow, and baking the dough on the end of a green stick. They ate the hot scones with dried buffalo meat. It was bitterly cold, rolled in their blankets and furs around the fire, but Dan had warmed large stones in it, and these they put into their sleeping sacks like hot warming pans.

Noon the next day found them concealed in snow-glopped pines looking down at a ranch in the valley below. Sergeant Farson passed his brass telescope to Pinkerton and said, 'Looks to me like there's just five men, and a couple of Indian hands.'

Through the glass Pinkerton focused on a corral at the side of the ranch house where the men appeared to be breaking horses. 'It's them,' he said, gleefully. 'That's definitely Frank Reno. I'm not sure about the others.'

'The one with the sideburns and forage cap, that's Charlie Spencer,' Tom Patterson muttered. 'And, yes, Miles Ogle, Albert Perkins, Mike Rogers. I don't recognize the big guy leaning on the corral rail.'

'Let's take a look.' Kilpatrick squinted through the telescope. 'That's Chuck Anderson. He ain't been with them long. He's wanted for robbery and homicide. This is the bunch we want.'

Sergeant Farson pondered the scene. 'These are dangerous men. My tactic would be to wait until before dawn, go in, take them by surprise.'

'We'll be frozen by then. My brain and body are numb already. Hoch!' Pinkerton gave a Glaswegian yell, his thin face splitting in a grin, fired with the spirit of Gaelic battles past. 'Let's go get 'em now.'

'As you like,' Sergeant Farson said, and checked his revolver. 'Mount up, men. Fire on my command. Or at will if we come under attack.'

'Charlie, why don't you stay up here with that Henry rifle of yourn? You can give 'em something to think about if they try to escape.'

The first Frank Reno knew, as he tried to rope a stallion, was a cry from one of his Indian wranglers, and looking round saw nine men ploughing their horses down the slope out of the trees towards them. 'Hell,' he whispered, 'who's this?' He breathed on his fingers to try to warm them, and reached for his Smith and Wesson. 'Don't take any nonsense. Shoot to kill, boys.'

'It's the mounties,' Mike Ogle cried, seeing a glimpse of red uniform through an open coat, as the horsemen came relentlessly on until they were nearly in handgun range. 'What do they want?'

'What the hell you think?' Charlie Spencer drawled. 'They ain't making a social visit.'

The horsemen had slowed to a halt as Sergeant Farson held up his right hand. The wind had dropped, there was a dead calm, and his voice rang out clearly. 'All you men are under arrest. I would advise you to come quietly.'

'Get lost,' Chuck Anderson growled. A burly, bearded man, he raised a heavy Volcanic and fired the first shot. The shot whistled past Farson, grazing his cheek, startling his horse.

'Charge!' Pinkerton hollered, his dander up, and he sent his mare plunging forward, exchanging shots with Anderson, fearless of his own danger.

Up on the hill Durango lined up his sights. 'The boss has gone crazy,' he said. 'They'll cut him down.' He squeezed the trigger, waiting only to see the bullet cut into Anderson's upper arm spurting blood, making him squeal and drop his gun. 'One fer the pot,' he grinned, levering another slug in.

The outlaws had backed away, taking advantage of cover of the corral gateposts, to set up a withering fusillade at the attackers. Pinkerton had charged past them, firing wildly from the saddle. He grabbed his carbine from the boot, jumped from his horse and took up a position behind a horse trough to attack them from the rear.

The mounties and his agents jumped from their horses, and attempted, on foot, to surround them, firing their revolvers as they dodged for cover. Spencer, Rogers, Ogle and Perkins were putting up a desperate resistance.

Frank Reno had quickly realized that it was time to run. 'Cut 'em down,' he shouted, and, opening the corral gate, leapt onto one of the horses, bareback, hanging low over its neck, galloping out through the gunfire as bullets whipped about him. He jumped down at the ranch house and ran inside.

'What's he up to?' Pinkerton gritted out. His horse had wandered off. He began to run towards the house on foot, but it was a good two hundred yards away, and, by now, Reno might well be covering him from a window. 'He ain't gonna get away this time.'

Reno, in fact, was in his office, desperately looting his safe, stuffing wads of cash into his pockets. He glanced, nervously, through a window. The battle outside was still going on. With any luck he might be able to make it back to Windsor. He ran out the back of the house, saddled a mustang in the barn, and charged out and away along the valley, whipping it mercilessly.

'He will, will he?' Durango muttered. There was only one way to stop him. He didn't want to, but needs be. He took careful aim with the Henry, squeezed the trigger and sent a slug big enough to bring a buffalo down spinning and whistling through the cold air. Reno was already half a mile from the house. The bullet ploughed into the mustang's heart, toppling him in his tracks, and Frank Reno was hurled over his head.

Charlie Durango didn't waste any time. He swung onto his bronc and went racing down the hillside towards the fallen rider. When he reached him Reno was groaning and concussed, getting to his feet. 'Howdy, Frank. We meet again. Remember what you did to me last time we met?' Durango swung his Henry rifle to crack the barrel across Reno's jaw, knocking him down again. 'Howdja like a taste of it?'

The men at the corral, out of ammunition, had surrendered by the time he got Reno back to the house. 'Here he is,' Charlie grinned, shoving Frank in before him. 'He's given us a fair old run for our money.'

Cash there was in plenty on Reno and in the house and they took it back to Windsor with them, leaving the two Indian boys to look after the stock. When they arrived back at the border there were paper formalities, but Sergeant Farson eased them through, with their bags of cash, which, he figured, must be the property of the railroad. He saluted their ferry boat, as it pulled out onto the choppy river to transport the Pinkerton men, and their prisoners, over to the other side.

Allan Pinkerton had cuffed himself to the wrist of Charlie Spencer, Kilpatrick to that of Miles Ogle, Patterson to Perkins, and Durango to Reno, while they kept the limping Anderson, and the runty Rogers in front of them.

At a time when men had been made instant millionaires through gold, silver, railroad speculation and cattle, fifty thousand dollars was not a vast fortune, comparatively, but it could grease an awful lot of palms, and word of Reno's capture had got out, and also rumour of the cash the agents were carrying.

The agents were feeling pretty pleased with themselves as they headed back, with their horses, on the thumping, creaking ferry boat. Suddenly, through the mist a steamboat tug approached. 'What's the matter with him?' Pinkerton yelled. 'He's coming straight at us.'

The iron bows of the tough little tugboat smashed into the wooden ferry and horses and men began to slide into the icy water. In the confusion the first thing Charlie Durango knew was a hard fist belonging to Frank Reno smashing into his face. Reno was trying to jump on board the tug, dragging Charlie with him.

The crunch to the jaw had put Durango's head into a spin, and he was unable to avoid being dragged over the side into the tug with Frank, who took the opportunity to whip Charlie's Paterson from his holster. He was bringing it up, pointing it at the agent's heart, as the tug turned back towards Canada through the swirling water. Charlie lunged his free hand to get a grip on the long barrel, thrusting it away.

As the two men on the tug struggled for possession of the revolver, the Pinkerton men had been thrown into the water, with their prisoners, from the sinking ferry. Manacled to three of them, struggling and cursing, they fought to keep their heads above the freezing waves. Fortunately, another steamboat heading up river had seen their plight, and drew alongside to haul them to safety.

On the tug, Durango was face to face with Frank Reno. Both strong men, it had become a match of wills to try to turn the revolver towards each other's body. At one point, the gleaming-eyed Frank had the barrel to Durango's cheek and crashed out a shot. But the boat lurched in the swell and the slug burned past his ear.

Durango brought his knee up hard, and Reno gasped. His face contorted with rage and pain, he tried to force the revolver back towards the agent's chest. Durango held onto the gun, and brought his manacled hand up, with Frank's in tow, to smash into the outlaw's face. He pounded him again and again, and Reno went down on his knees. Charlie wrested his gun from his hand and found himself in charge of the situation. He dragged Reno with him to the wheelhouse and put the Paterson to the temple of the tugboat man. 'Head back to the

American shore,' he growled.

By the time Pinkerton and his agents had dried out, had been put ashore with their prisoners, Charlie had deposited Frank in the local jail and caught the horses that had swum ashore. The thousands of dollars in their saddle-bags were stuck together in clammy wads, but he guessed they could be salvaged. Charlie was warming himself with a bottle of whiskey by the stove in the sheriff's office when his friends arrived. 'What took you so long?' he drawled.

In the morning they loaded their prisoners on board a locomotive headed towards New Albany. 'Well, Frank,' Charlie said, as he sat beside him, his rifle between his knees. 'I figure you should soon be joining your brother John on Rikers Island. I reckon they'll give you forty years hard labour.'

Frank Reno didn't reply, staring sourly out of the window as, eventually, they went rattling through Seymour.

'Was that your galfriend in the garden

hangin' out her washing?'

'Go to hell.'

'However did she get mixed up with a fella like you?' Charlie mused. 'But I guess you must have something.'

Reno spat on the agent's boot for reply.

'Hey, that ain't nice.'

14

They had made themselves comfortable in their cell on the landing of the fine new brick jailhouse in New Albany, Frank, William and Simeon Reno sharing a cell with Miles Ogle, their bunks double-banked. On 10 December they heard news that the railroad conductor, Jesse Bean, had finally died of his gunshot wounds.

'Too bad,' growled Frank, 'but they can't pin that on us. Abel Finnegan did it and he's already been lynched.'

He was still attired in his neat gambler's clothes, sporting his jutting beard, his black hair plastered down with oil. He tried to appear at ease as he spread a deck of cards, but, nonetheless, the news seemed to have made him nervous. He sprang up and shouted along to Charlie Spencer, Chuck Anderson, Rogers, and Perkins in the next cell. 'When we gonna bust outa this place? I wanna be home for Christmas.'

'Beats me,' Spencer sighed. 'That Tom Stone, he runs a tight jail.'

All their efforts at bribing Stone and his guards had fallen on deaf ears. They were kept in high security and it was difficult to get messages out to any supporters they might have. Stone kept a wary eye on them.

'We ain't got much time,' Frank said. 'We're due for trial in a week's time.'

'How long you think we'll get, Frank?' William whined for the umpteenth time.

'Aw, you boys won't get long. Maybe ten years at most. You'll still be young when you come out. Anyhow, I figure Clinton and the rest of the boys'll bust us out of here 'fore then.'

★ ★ ★

At midnight twelve men gathered at Seymour railroad depot. They wore pointed red hoods, the long capes coming down to disguise their clothes. Each had a number sewn in white on his back. They walked into the depot, ordered the conductor on duty to halt the night train with his flashlamp.

'What's going on?' the engineer called, as The Flyer came steaming in to an unscheduled stop.

'We're taking over,' one of the vigilantes said, stepping up onto the footplate, and pointing the business end of a carbine out from beneath his cloak. 'We've cut the telegraph lines. Nobody ain't gonna stop us.

When The Flyer rolled into New Albany a while later they left two of their men to cut the wires at that end and guard the passengers and any protesting railroadmen. 'Forward,' Number One shouted out. 'This is our night of revenge.'

Charlie Durango had been visiting the jail to serve papers on the prisoners, and had stayed, after splitting a bottle with the sheriff, putting his feet up in an office chair, while Tom Stone slept on his bunk. Suddenly, he heard the tramping of feet along the sidewalk and woke, scratching himself. 'Who the hell's that?'

Stone had rolled out of his bunk and went to peer out of the barred window. He saw the body of men in red masks approaching and his face tensed. 'It ain't nobody. Just some fellas been havin' a party, I guess.' He looked at his watch in the lamplight. It was two in the morning.

There was a hammering on the barred and bolted doors. Charlie sprang to his feet. 'What's happening?'

'Take it easy.' Stone had begun to unlock with considerable alacrity, opening the doors and saying, 'What do you fellas want?'

It seemed to Durango the sheriff was mighty quick to open up to strangers in the middle of the night, and when he saw the masked vigilantes pushing into the office, and Stone stepping aside, putting his hands up, he went for his Paterson, dragging it out from his holster and cocking it in the same motion. He was too late. A shot from the carbine of Number Three hammered into his shoulder with excruciating pain and sent him toppling to the floor.

'Take their guns, Number Eight, and put them in a cell. Number Four, get the sheriff's keys.'

'They're over on the hook,' Stone mumbled, as the groaning Durango was hauled into a cell.

'Where are they?'

'The last cell on the landing.'

Stone was shoved in with Charlie, the cell locked, and Number One led his men up the spiral iron staircase. He carried a hurricane lamp and shone it into each cell they passed. The prisoners were getting to their feet and calling out, wondering what was going on. Some drew back in terror when they saw the hooded men. Number One paused at the next-to-last cell. It was unlocked, and he pointed a finger at big Chuck Anderson, who was in his flannel long johns. 'He's to go.' Anderson began to struggle, but a carbine jammed into his belly told him it was not a good idea.

For moments, as he was woken, Frank Reno had a spurt of hope. 'They've come to get us out.' He heard Charlie Spencer next door cry out, 'Do you want me?' And his heart fell.

'No, not this time,' a muffled voice said. 'Just be warned, that's all. We're here for the Renos.'

Frank's throat went dry when he heard the sepulchral voices echoing around the landing, saw the door unlocked, the phantom-like men in their crimson hoods staring in at him, holding already-knotted hangman's nooses. 'No,' he croaked. It was the fate he had always dreaded, a hempen necktie. 'No, boys, please, don't do this.'

Simeon and William started weeping, screaming and begging as they were dragged out onto the landing. 'I'm too young to die,' Simeon cried. 'I didn't kill anybody.'

The ropes were tied tight to the landing rail as the other prisoners watched, horrified. The two younger Renos were hauled up, quivering and pleading, and the struggling Chuck Anderson cursed as he was forced to sit beside them, his arms gripped by the vigilantes. Nooses were placed over their heads.

Number One spoke, 'You are all unanimously condemned. Have you any last words?'

There was no reply, so he gave the signal. Will, Sim and Chuck were hurled out into space, brought to a stop with a jerk to kick air.

Frank Reno held up a hand as he came from the cell. He was in a white shirt and trousers, his feet bare. 'All right,' he said, peering down at his brothers twisting on their ropes. He climbed onto the rail. 'Don't push me. I'll do it myself. Just give me a few minutes.' He sat like a diver on a board, looking down. 'Tell Hetty I'm sorry,' he whispered, and leaped into eternity.

There was a sigh of awe from the watching prisoners in their cells. Miles Ogle, Perkins and Rogers, cowered back, stunned that they had not been summoned, too.

'By this act we hope to have rooted out evil,' Number One intoned. 'Let all be warned.' Below him the four men swung.

He turned and led his masked followers out of the jail. The Flyer was hissing and steaming, held there by the two armed vigilantes. It was 2.30 a.m. 'You will take us back to Seymour,' Number Eight told the driver. 'Then you are free to go on your way.'

At Seymour the vigilantes left the train and melted into the night.

★ ★ ★

Charlie Durango was sitting up in bed some weeks later in his hotel room, his chest bandaged, recuperating from his injury. There was a knock on the door and he reached for his Paterson, calling out, 'It's open.'

'Don't shoot me,' Hetty said. 'I've come to see how you are.'

She sat on a chair by his bed as he put the revolver aside. She had a hatbox in her hands, which she offered him.

'What is it?' He took out his tall-crowned, somewhat battered Capper and Capper. 'Hey, my hat!'

'It was hanging on the peg in the saloon,' she smiled.

'You ain't upset . . . about Frank?'

'Well, of course.' She made a down-turned grimace and gave a shudder. 'It was an awful way to go. But I guess I knew one day it would end like that.'

He shoved fingers through his thick white hair, clearing it from his dark, chiselled face, which creased into a grin as his grey eyes twinkled. 'You look pretty as a picture. You don't know what it does for me seein' you again.'

Hetty was wearing a checked cape over her high-throated dress, her hands in a fur muff against the cold. She had a large hat with what looked like a small windmill on it. 'I made it for one of the girls,' she said, smiling, seeing his glance. 'But they've all gone. We've got a decent God-fearing town now.'

'What happened to Abe Wappenshaw?'

'They stripped him of his badge, tarred and feathered him, ran him out of town. We're looking for a lawman. I've come to ask if you'll take the job.'

'I dunno.' Charlie's broad, bronzed shoulders were leaned back against the bedhead. 'How about persuadin' me?'

Hetty rose to sit on the bed beside him. She leaned forward and gently kissed his lips, his moustache tickling her nose. 'Would that help?'

'That sure did,' he said, as she drew away. 'But if I was sheriff of Seymour I'd have to investigate those men, the vigilance committee, for committing those illegal murders. It wouldn't be hard to track 'em down, especially the one with the blood red boots, the gold signet ring and the hoity way of talking. I don't want to do that. What's done's done.'

'So, what are you going to do?'

'Allen Pinkerton's asked me to be his top man out in Denver. Colorado's fine country. Maybe in a few years I could retire, raise a few cows. It's lonesome territory. Man needs a wife along.'

'Are you asking me to be — ?'

'What else?'

'I will. On one condition. You get rid of that moustache.'

'Aw, I couldn't do that,' he drawled. 'It's my trademark.'

'Oh, well, I guess I'll just have to accept your imperfections,' she said and hugged herself into him. 'Like you'll have to accept mine.'

'Ouch,' he said. 'Mind my shoulder. That hurts.'

★ ★ ★

In Seymour, when Hetty returned to pack up her things, a large printed notice had been tacked to the wall of the saloon. It was headed, 'Headquarters, Vigilance Committee — *Salus populi suprema lex*,' and in verbose flowery language regretted the recent tragedy at New Albany, ending, 'We are loath to shed blood again and will not do so unless compelled in defence of our lives.'

A 'warning' was issued to 'any of the remaining thieves, their friends and sympathizers, who have threatened vengeance, including Clinton Reno, Trick Reno, Wilk Reno, Fee Johnson, Billy Biggers, Jesse Thompson . . . If these individuals desire to remain in our midst to pursue honest callings and conduct themselves as law-abiding citizens we will protect them. If, however, they commence their devilish designs against us, our property, or any good citizens of this district, we will rise but *once* more. Do not trifle with us, for if you do, we will follow you to the bitter end and give you short shrift and a hempen collar.

By order of the Committee.'

THE END